NEW YORK REVIEW BOOKS

CLASSICS

THE PILGRIM HAWK

GLENWAY WESCOTT (1901–1987) grew up in Wisconsin, but moved to France with his companion Monroe Wheeler in 1925. Wescott's early fiction, notably the stories in *Goodbye, Wisconsin* and the novel *The Grandmothers* (in which Alwyn Tower, the narrator of *The Pilgrim Hawk*, makes his first appearance), were set in his native Midwest. Later work included essays on political, literary, and spiritual subjects, as well as the novels *The Pilgrim Hawk* and *Apartment in Athens*. Wescott's journals, recording his many literary and artistic friendships and offering an intimate view of his life as a gay man, were published posthumously under the title *Continual Lessons*.

MICHAEL CUNNINGHAM is the author of three novels, *A Home at the End of the World*, *Flesh and Blood*, and *The Hours*, which won the 1999 Pulitzer Prize in Fiction.

THE
PILGRIM HAWK
A LOVE STORY

Glenway Wescott

■

Introduction by

MICHAEL CUNNINGHAM

NEW YORK REVIEW BOOKS

New York

THIS IS A NEW YORK REVIEW BOOK
PUBLISHED BY THE NEW YORK REVIEW OF BOOKS

This edition published in 2001 in the United States of America by
The New York Review of Books, 1755 Broadway New York, NY 10019

Library of Congress Cataloging-in-Publication Data
Wescott, Glenway, 1901-
  The pilgrim hawk : a love story / Glenway Wescott.
    p. cm.
  ISBN 0-940322-56-0
  1. Americans—France—Fiction. 2. Irish—France—Fiction. 3.
Novelists—Fiction. 4. France—Fiction. 5. Hawks—Fiction. I. Title.
  PS3545.E827 P5 2001
  813'.52—dc21

                        00-011548

ISBN 0-940322-56-0

Book designed by Red Canoe, Deer Lodge, Tennessee
Caroline Kavanagh, Deb Koch
Printed in the United States of America on acid-free paper.
10 9 8 7 6 5 4 3 2 1

January 2001
www.nybooks.com

For Nelson
March to July, 1940;
Stone-blossom and New York

INTRODUCTION

We may consider Glenway Wescott's *The Pilgrim Hawk* to be a short novel or a long novella, but whatever we choose to call it, it is exactly as long as it needs to be. It is murderously precise and succinct. It contains, in its 108 pages, more levels and layers of experience than many books five times its length.

The book centers on various overlapping triangles among a group of beings who are mostly, but not exclusively, human. It takes place during a single summer afternoon in the late 1920s in a French country house, where Alexandra Henry, the young American heiress who owns it, is entertaining an American house guest named Alwyn Tower, the book's narrator. On this particular afternoon Alexandra and Tower are visited by the Cullens, a wealthy Irish couple who, in their ongoing and rather aimless travels, are en route to Budapest in a Daimler, driven by their young chauffeur. Larry Cullen is, or at least appears to be, the very image of the hale, silly aristocrat. His wife, Madeleine, is an aging beauty who has spent her marriage dragging her husband through one rough devotion after another, most of them involving radical Irish politics or the killing of some wild animal, and who appears at the château with her latest enthusiasm, a hawk she is training to hunt. She has named the hawk Lucy, after the Walter Scott and Donizetti heroine, and she wears it perched on her wrist like a sacred jewel.

At the same time a parallel story transpires in the kitchen, involving Ricketts, the chauffeur, and Alexandra's servants, Jean and Eva, a husband and wife from Morocco. These seven characters—eight if we include the hawk, and we must include the hawk—are the novel's entire population. From this small cast of characters, in the course of what should be an innocuous interlude of cocktails and dinner, Wescott summons a series of revelations that doesn't stop until the book's ambiguous, quietly lethal last lines.

Beyond that, I see no point in a detailed synopsis. Suffice it to say that *The Pilgrim Hawk* is an endlessly intricate meditation on freedom versus captivity and passion versus peace, among other subjects; and that in terms of character and event it is strung throughout with little bombs, some of which explode on contact, some considerably later. Rendered geometrically, the novel's structure might resemble a series of intersecting triangles canted at various angles in space, irregular but perfect, in the way of quartz crystals. With its single bucolic setting and the desperate, strangling wit and manners of its most prominent characters, it owes a good deal to Chekhov. Wescott shares with Chekhov an insistence that the enormous is amply contained within the small; that the ingredients of tragedy can be found in abundance among genteel, indolent people passing an afternoon together in a parlor and a garden.

All that occurs in *The Pilgrim Hawk* takes place within the borders of this miniature world. The action does not extend beyond the house and grounds—even the book's one incident of physical violence takes place outside our range of vision. The whole story could be presented on stage with almost no alterations. Its static quality is, however, by no means accidental. The narrative is restricted in the way that the bird (and the people) are confined. As the story progresses we learn that every domesticated hawk has been captured in the wild, since hawks do not mate or breed in captivity. "They never get over being wild," as Mrs.

Cullen says, and though trained hawks could always choose to fly away when hunting, they do not, she explains, because in captivity "it's a better life, more food and more fun."

Some readers may groan inwardly, as I did, when I first read about the hawk. Oh, I thought, a symbol. And the hawk is, of course, a symbol—hawks are members of a small category of creatures and objects that can't be anything but symbols when they appear in books. However, if novelists are determined, as they should be, to write about everything in the world, it is just as important to find new life in the old images as it is to invent new ones. Wescott knew what he was up against, what sort of portentousness he flirted with, and it is a measure of his talent that he was able not only to fully engage what might be implied by such a stubbornly meaningful image but also to create a hawk that is, apart from its larger meaning, an entirely convincing, integral member of the story. Wescott was a man who had *looked* at hawks:

> [The hawk's] body was as long as her mistress's arm; the wing feathers in repose a little too long, slung across her back like a folded tent. . . . Her luxurious breast was white, with little tabs or tassels of chestnut. Out of tasseled pantaloons

her legs came down straight to the perch with no apparent flesh on them, enameled a greenish yellow.

But her chief beauty was that of expression. It was like a little flame; it caught and compelled your attention like that, although it did not flicker and there was nothing bright about it nor any warmth in it. It is a look that men sometimes have; men of great energy, whose appetite or vocation has kept them absorbed every instant all their lives. They may be good men but they are often mistaken for evil men, and vice versa. In Lucy's case it appeared chiefly in her eyes, not black but funereally brown, and extravagantly large, set deep in her flattened head.

The hawk's wonderfully drawn wildness—its profound otherness—slices like a razor through the world of indolent expatriate luxury in which the book is set, some years before the Second World War, which will not only send Alwyn Tower and Alexandra Henry fleeing back to America but will extinguish a certain lazy, genteel optimism; a belief in the relative sanctity of hedges and lawns as well as a more general belief in our collective ability to select and enforce happy endings. The book declares itself at the start to be set in a less difficult past; to be both lit and obscured by wistfulness. We learn, through Mrs. Cullen, that only captive hawks have any chance of living out their natural spans—in the wild they always die of starvation, when they grow too old to hunt—and as we read we pick up stray fragments about the loneliness and failure that await some of the characters as certainly as war awaits the world in which they live. Most significantly we receive, in the opening line, an offhand and all but invisible reference to what the future holds for Tower and Alexandra, though we are not permitted to understand what their futures imply until we reach the story's end.

Every character proves, by the book's close, to be more than he or she first seemed to be, just as every relationship turns out to be far more complex and perverse than we might have imagined at the outset. This is most conspicuously true of the Cullens, whom we meet as relatively standard-issue eccentrics, two of the wealthy, outdoorsy people Alexandra has coped with all her privileged life, "self-centered but without any introspection, strenuous but emotionally idle." By the end of the quietly calamitous afternoon, superficial Cullen is revealed as a tragic and potentially dangerous figure, driven to extremes by a jealousy broad and deep enough to include a bird. Mrs. Cullen metamorphoses from a chilly matron into a rough, wild Irish girl grown old and, finally, into something like an Amazon. As she tries to retrieve the hawk after it has escaped we see that

> that French or Italian footwear of hers with three-inch heels not only incapacitated her but flattered her, and disguised her. Now her breasts seemed lower on her torso, out of the way of her nervous arms. Her hips were wide and her back powerful, with that curve from the shoulder blades to the head which you see in the nudes of Ingres. She walked with her legs well apart, one padding foot-fall after another, as impossible to trip up as a cat.

The book treats the parallel drama among Jean, Eva, and Ricketts as peripheral—they live in the novel as they live in the households of Alexandra and the Cullens: in cars and kitchens, out of the way. They are, of course, captives themselves, and they matter more or less the way wild pets matter: as curiosities, as sources of trouble, and, more obscurely, as subjugated invaders from a realm of frighteningly rampant desires. Wescott chose to depict his vanishing world from the point of view of those who are served, and to let the servers remain as obscure to the reader as they are to their keepers. The story immerses us not only in a world but in a particular way of living in that world. Jean, Eva, and the chauffeur, like the titular hawk, play crucial roles in the stories of the wealthy but exist in a world of their own as well. One imagines they pass through this novel while living out an unwritten novel of their own, one in which they are the central figures, and the commotion created by those people in the parlor is important but secondary.

At the center of the story, omnipresent but also concealed, is Alwyn Tower himself, and he proves to be the darkest and most surprising figure of all. Tower lives within the confines of his own domesticity more or less as the hawk does, for similar reasons—it's a better life, more food and more fun—and probably at similar cost, though Wescott is too subtle to offer a mere plea, in narrative form, for freedom over captivity. Tower is not yet old but is no longer young. He is trying, and failing, to write novels, and he has been in love twice, though we learn nothing of the particulars in either case. (In one of the book's many symmetries we are told that trained hawks can only tolerate two consecutive unsuccessful strikes before they despair and fly away, to a freedom that will eventually starve them to death.) Tower is essentially an engine of perception, of exquisitely cruel and precise judgments.

Although he has failed at writing he is, in a sense, the very embodiment of the novelist, who must of necessity see more than his characters see, know more about them than they can know about themselves. If this is a requisite virtue in a novelist, however, it is a fatal flaw in a life being lived. Tower sees too much and, in seeing so clearly, wants too little. He could be a character from Greek myth: a man so gifted with vision that he is unable to abandon it and simply, irrationally desire anyone or anything. In the book, Tower is, as he would wish to be, barely perceptible, except through the workings of his exquisite eye.

The same might be said of Wescott the novelist, whose eye is so cold and precise, so hawklike, that the novel itself might suffer from an excess of clarity and a dearth of passion if it weren't redeemed by its language. Almost every page contains some small wonder of phrase or insight, some instance of the world keenly observed and reinvented. Of hunters near Alexandra's château, Wescott writes, "We could hear their hunting horns which sounded like a picnic of boy sopranos, lost." When Mrs. Cullen gives Tower the hawk to hold, briefly, on his wrist, we read, "At the least move her talons pricked the leather and pulled it a bit—as fashionable women's fingernails do on certain fabrics—though evidently she held them as loose and harmless as she could. Only her grip as a whole was hard, like a pair of tight, heated iron bracelets." Sentences like that are beauties in themselves, and the fact that they also serve the book's larger meanings can only be considered with an appreciation bordering on awe.

To my mind, *The Pilgrim Hawk* stands unembarrassed beside Ford Madox Ford's *The Good Soldier*, F. Scott Fitzgerald's *The Great Gatsby*, and Henry James's "The Aspern Papers." Those particular titles come to mind because they are all stories about disastrously intense passions and desires, narrated by someone untroubled by either, or, at best, by passions and desires that prove disastrously easy to manage. Each book offers, in one way or another, a narrative keyhole through which the reader is invited to peer at scandalous and salacious acts, and each implies that whatever cannot be seen through the keyhole is at least as significant as what can. Finally, each shares the conviction that, as far as human affairs are concerned, it may be better to live hugely and tragically, even in the service of some grand, ardent mistake, than submit to the seductions of mildness, reason, and order.

It is James, however, whom Wescott most nearly resembles. Ford and Fitzgerald produce their internal combustions at least in part by subjecting cosseted characters to ordained accidents, by creating collisions between comfort and chaos, but Wescott, like James, produces all his sparks from within: what fascinates him are devastating events that spring directly from character. *The Pilgrim Hawk* could be the work of a particularly brilliant clockmaker—a clockmaker capable of creating a mechanism of gears, springs, and pulleys that, when set in motion, obeys every known law of cause and effect but results, ultimately, in chaos. There is a sense, in Wescott as in James, that the mechanism requires no outside intervention: no matter how many times we wind the clock it will always tick along, with flawless precision, toward the same undoing.

The Pilgrim Hawk is, in short, a work of brilliance, and brilliance is not a work one often gets to apply to obscure books more than sixty years old. It was Wescott's second novel, following his well-received book *The Grandmothers*. He would publish one more, *Apartment in Athens*, in 1945, and then live another forty years publishing only essays and journals. There is, to my knowledge, little information about why he stopped writing fiction, though I tend to believe that writers who stop writing do so for reasons as ultimately mysterious as those that drove them to attempt writing in the first place. Whether the general neglect of Wescott's book stems from his long period of relative silence, or from the book's foreignness (it is a profoundly European book written by an American, and difficult to categorize), its stern and rather drab title (one wonders what would have happened to *The Great Gatsby* if Fitzgerald had obeyed his early inclination to call it *The High-Bouncing Lover*), or some more fundamental flaw in the world's ability to keep track of its gifts and glories, I can't help but believe that it will not only survive but, ultimately, prosper. Those of us who love books, as well as those of us who write them, are sometimes called upon for prodigious acts of patience.

—MICHAEL CUNNINGHAM

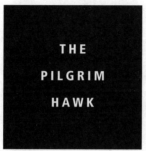

THE
PILGRIM
HAWK

THE CULLENS WERE Irish; but it was in France that I met them and was able to form an impression of their love and their trouble. They were on their way to a property they had rented in Hungary; and one afternoon they came to Chancellet to see my great friend Alexandra Henry. That was in May of 1928 or 1929, before we all returned to America, and she met my brother and married him.

Needless to say, the twenties were very different from the thirties, and now the forties have begun. In the twenties it was not unusual to meet foreigners in some country as foreign to them as to you, your pere- grination just crossing theirs; and you did your best to know them in an afternoon or so; and perhaps you called that little lightning knowledge, friendship. There was a kind of idealistic or optimistic curiosity in the air. And vagaries of character, and the various war and peace that goes on in the psyche, seemed of the greatest interest and even importance.

Chancellet must be a painful place in the forties, although one of the least changed in France, I suppose, because it is unimportant. As I remember, there was a school of what is now romantically called celestial navigation, with a modest flying field and a few hangars, two or three kilometers away, at Pelors; but if that is in use now the foreigners must have it. In our day, day in and day out, the old Duchesse de Challot and her poor relations and friends in tight coats on wind-broken mounts used to hunt in the forest of Pelors. We could hear their hunting horns which sounded like a picnic of boy sopranos, lost. Meanwhile perhaps there have been anti-aircraft guns for the defense of Paris embedded all amid the earths of foxes: angry radio stammering in the well-kept branches. Now at least the foxes and the thrushes can come back. The old ex-cabinet-minister whose château and little park adjoined Alex's garden is dead.

Her house was just a section of the village street: two small dwellings and a large horse-stable combined and rebuilt and expensively furnished in the plain modern style. She or her architect made a mistake in the planning of the ground floor. The dining room and the chief guest-room were on the street, which is also the highway to Orléans and the tourist country of the Loire; so that the reckless French traffic practically brushed the walls, and heavy trucks alarmed one all night. Not only Alex's bedroom but the kitchen and pantry opened into the spacious and quiet garden. This delighted the new servants whom Alex had brought up from Morocco, a romantic pair named Jean and Eva. They promptly took a far corner of it under some plane trees for their own use; and all spring they passed every spare moment there, quarreling and occasionally weeping during the day, but like clockwork making peace and sealing it with kisses in the twilight or moonlight . . . I mention this odd location of the servants' quarters because, that afternoon of the Cullens' visit, I went to speak to Jean and happened to look out the kitchen window and saw Cullen in the garden, futilely giving way to his awful jealousy, emancipated from love for a few minutes.

There had been no mention of their coming, or perhaps I had forgotten it. I heard the doorbell ring, then ring again. Jean and Eva must have been outdoors or napping. Alex had put through a telephone call to London upon some little annoying matter of business, and wished not to be disturbed. So I went to the door; and there was the long dark Daimler entirely occupying the cobbled space between the house and the highway, and there stood the Irishman about to ring a third time. "Oh, how d'ya do, is this Miss Henry's house, my name's Cullen," he said; and turned to help Mrs. Cullen out of the car, which was a delicate operation, for she bore a full-grown hooded falcon on her wrist. A dapper young chauffeur also helped. She was dressed with extreme elegance and she wore the highest heels I ever saw, on which, with one solicitous male at each elbow, she stumbled across the ancient cobblestones, the bird swaying a little and hunching its wings to steady itself.

I told them my name, and they repeated it after me and shook hands with a somewhat grand and vague affability. "I brought my hawk," Mrs. Cullen unnecessarily announced. "She's new. I thought Alex wouldn't mind. And I hope you too," she added and paused a moment, with bright eyes to flatter me just in case I felt entitled to authority of some sort in Alex's house, "I hope you won't mind." She had no way of knowing who or what I was: casual caller or one of Alex's kinsmen or perhaps a sweetheart.

Her eyes were a crystal blue, unmistakably Irish; and she was unmistakable in other ways too, in spite of her brisk London voice and fine French dress. Her make-up was better than you would have expected of a lady falconer; still you could see that her skin was naturally downy and her snub nose tended to be pink. There was also a crookedness, particularly in the alignment of her nostrils and her voluble little lips. How rare pulchritude is among the Irish, I said to myself; therefore what a trouble is made when it does appear: Emer and Deirdre, Mrs. O'Shea and Mrs. McBride. Then my glance fell upon Mrs. Cullen's snowy dimpled fingers, with a considerable diamond on one, a star sapphire on another. Between her sleeve and the rough gauntlet to which the falcon clung, her wrist showed like a bit of Easter lily; and her ankle was a match for it, perfectly straight in a mere glimmer of stocking. No doubt these fine points were enough to entitle her to a certain enchantment and disturbance of the opposite sex: her husband for one.

Meanwhile Jean had come running in a fine embarrassment, buttoning his white jacket; and I sent him to inform his mistress of the arrival of her guests and to guide their chauffeur to the garage, while I tried to usher them into the living room. But Mrs. Cullen went on explaining the hawk. "Her name's Lucy. Don't you think she's sweet? She's Scottish; I've only had her five or six weeks. A gamekeeper near

Inverness trapped her, but she's all right, only one toe bent in the trap. D'you see, this toe?" She paused on the threshold and held up the gloved hand and wrist on which Lucy perched, and I saw: gripping the rugged and stained leather, one sharp talon that did not grip straight. The stain on the leather was dried blood.

"I call her Lucy because my old father used to make me read Scott to him in the winter whenever the weather got too beastly to hunt. I thought Alex would like to see her."

"We had to bring her anyway," her husband loudly chimed in. "The most awful things happen if we leave her in the hotel. She frightens the chambermaids, and they scream and weep. I have to give immense tips."

He was a large man, not really fat but with bulk and softness irregularly here and there, not so much in the middle as up and down his back, all around his head, in his hands. His British complexion suggested eating and drinking rather than hunting and shooting; certainly nothing about him suggested hawking. His hazel eyes were a little bloodshot, wavering golden now and then; and he had a way of opening and shutting his lips, like an unsympathetic pout, or a dispirited kiss, under the tufts of his mustache.

We were about to sit down in the living room when they both noticed it, and evidently felt obliged to comment. "What a splendid room, splendid," they said; "most unusual and modern and comfortable." It was not splendid, but it was very large: the entire former stable with the hayloft removed so that the roof constituted the ceiling, with old chestnut rafters gothically pointing up twenty-five or thirty feet; the woodwork darkly waxed and the walls painted white. It reminded me of a village church. At regular intervals all around hung certain modern pictures with only blunt rudimentary drawing and overflowing color, like stained glass. But on as fine a day as this, modern art was dimmed and dwarfed by the view of the garden and the park beyond it, Alex's architect having removed almost a third of the wall on that side and put in two great panes of plate glass.

Mrs. Cullen tripped over to this great window and courteously exclaimed once more: "Splendid garden. What luck to have a pond!" It was what the French call an English garden; no formal flower beds—a few blossoms amid the grass, paths along the water, and shrubs flourishing, in the muffled brilliance of late May. The characteristic Seine-et-Oise sky, foamy cloud and weak blue, lay at our feet also, daubed in a soft copy on the surface of the pond. In the background every tree was draped in a slightly different shade of the same ecstatic color.

But as Mrs. Cullen stood facing all this, I had an impression of indifference and mere courtesy; her look did not take in much. A little narrow frown, an efficient survey, only to discover if there was anything in it for her personally; and there was not. In a moment the light eyelashes began to flutter again, and the blue pupils loosened, merely sparkling. Her prolonged and expressive looks were all for her husband or her hawk.

Now, what seeing the garden chiefly reminded her of was that the hawk could not see: its entire head except the beak encased in its plumed Dutch hood. "Poor Lucy, blind as a bat," she murmured; and very deftly, taking one drawstring in her teeth and the other between thumb and forefinger of her right hand, she unhooded it. It also frowned, and stared circularly at the room and blinked at the window. Then it opened out and rearranged the whitish and bluish feathers around its throat; combed its head between its tethered legs; smoothed its cheek against its powerful shoulder.

Mrs. Cullen paced up and down, evidently trying to decide which armchair would suit her and Lucy best. Then Alex came in from her long-distance business, with apologies for not welcoming them at once. They replied with another round of compliments upon the house and garden, and there was a new introduction of the falcon. "Lucy, for Lucy Ashton, Lucy of Lammermoor," Mrs. Cullen explained. "Don't you remember her song? *Easy live and quiet die, Vacant hand and heart and eye.*"

To my amusement Cullen hummed a few notes of the Mad Scene from *Lucia* in a manly Irish treble. His wife hushed him by murmuring his name, which was Larry; and went on informing Alex that they were at the Plaza-Honoré, busy shopping in Paris, eager to leave for Hungary via Strasbourg on the morrow. I was impatient for them to cease this small talk and be seated, because I wanted to sit down and admire the falcon comfortably, and to ask certain questions. At last Mrs. Cullen requested a straight chair, which I brought from the dining room.

I was much impressed by Alex's enthusiasm during this first part of the Cullens' visit. It reminded me that she must be lonely here in France with only myself and my cousin and a few other friends rather like us. She had spent a number of years in Scotland with her father, and in Morocco, and journeying around the Orient; and in London also the acquaintances of her girlhood had been outdoor people like these two, self-centered but without any introspection, strenuous but emotionally idle. It was a type of humanity that she no longer quite respected or trusted, but evidently still enjoyed.

Their enthusiasm about themselves and all that exactly appertained to them, always overflowing, coolly playing and bubbling over in mild agitation like a fountain, held your attention and mirrored itself in your mind; little by little you began to bubble with it. One of Alex's obvious characteristics was lack of curiosity; and I think that was chiefly fear of arousing or authorizing others' inquiry about herself. Perhaps selfishness reassured her and made her less shy. In any case, that afternoon she eagerly asked questions, including some that I had in mind; and Mrs. Cullen was charmed to answer; and Cullen was charmed to listen and give back his approximate echoes. Thus an odd kind of compatibility was established, in which I too gradually let myself be included, somewhat to my surprise.

For one thing, the bird charmed me so that nothing else mattered much. And it served as an embodiment or emblem for me of all the truly interesting subjects of conversation that these very sociable, traveling, sporting people leave out as a rule: illness, poverty, sex, religion, art. Whenever I began to be bored, a solemn glance of its maniacal eyes helped me to stop listening and to think concentratedly of myself instead, or for myself.

Furthermore the Cullens began to puzzle me, to charm me in that sense. Whether or not I finally arrive at a proper understanding of people, I often begin in the way of a vexed, intense superficiality. And indeed they were mere male and female of that species of well-to-do British which haunts the entire world with excess of energy and sedate manner. They were self-absorbed, coldly gregarious, mere passers of time. But nothing about them was authentically sedate or even peaceful. There Cullen plumply sat in Alex's softest armchair, his legs more widely spread or loosely crossed than you would expect of a conventional gentleman; licking his lips under his fringy mustache; evidently thinking of his dinner; interrupting his wife's conversation at regular intervals as if that were his life work. Yet he seemed to be constantly fighting against some strange feeling, and to be somehow outwitted by it. Whenever he spoke, his wife smiled or at least tilted her head toward him. This, I felt, was chiefly good breeding on her part; many of his remarks, and especially his tone of voice, seemed unpleasant. But between remarks, in her glances at him, there was affection as bright as tears. And during the loving fuss she made over the great bird on her arm, she kept shifting her eyes in his direction, imploring him to try to like it too. It might have been a baby, and he a lover; or was it the other way around?

Alex expressed surprise that they should willingly

leave Ireland at this lovely time of year. Mrs. Cullen answered that, in season or out, there was nothing much to do in Ireland except hunt. "And our terrible sons pinch our hunters when they come home. We can't afford to keep enough for them. I can't bear a horse that others have been riding."

She also alluded mildly to the diminishment of the old quiet kind of fortune like theirs. The banshee in the drafty corridor or the weedy hedge crying not the deaths of relatives but increase of taxes, decrease of rents and investments . . . Indeed they still appeared rich, in hand-woven silk with diamonds, in tweed as soft as silk, stopping at the Plaza-Honoré, en route to Budapest in a Daimler. But all that in fact is cheaper than an old country house full of guests, and the requisite stable and kennel and larder and cellar, and servants enough. Having closed Cullen Hall, Mrs. Cullen pointed out, they were in a position to accept invitations half the year; and the continent was cheap.

Evidently her telling us this vexed Cullen. He warmly informed us that one of his neighbors, a drunken idiot anyway, had sold everything that the entail permitted, and two of his cousins were obliged to rent; and so it went all over the British Isles. Their own circumstances were neither discreditable nor hopeless. There were still certain inheritances due them, on his side, not Mrs. Cullen's. His sons might be considered grown men, except by their mother; but they were still engaged in that great postponement, education, which is expensive. His brother and sister were happy to have them during their long vacations; but as a rule they preferred to loiter at Cullen Hall with two or three servants who were too old to dismiss anyway; and they hunted with the neighbors. It is easy for youngsters to get on with new people, even such as the latest in their county, a manufacturing peer named Bild, a Jew; not at all easy for him.

Mrs. Cullen said a word in defense of Lord Bild. Thank heaven it was he who had bought the estate adjoining Cullen Hall, on their youngsters' account especially. Although of common Germanic origin he was very strict about manners and sportsmanship and keeping fit; more so than they were. Neighborly influence is like education; the best teachers belong to the races and classes which have been learning themselves just lately.

Now Cullen had risen and was standing at his wife's elbow, shaking his finger at the falcon teasingly. I thought that the bird's great eyes showed only a slight natural bewilderment; whereas a slow sneer came over his face and he turned pale. It was the first revelation I had of the interesting fact that he hated Lucy.

He would willingly have sacrificed a finger tip in order to have an excuse to retaliate, I thought; and I imagined him picking up a chair or a coffee table and going at her with smashing blows. What a difference there is between animals and humans! Lucy no doubt would be disgustingly fierce when her time came; but meanwhile sat pleasantly and idly, in abeyance. Whereas humanity is histrionic, and must prepare and practice every stroke of passion; so half our life is vague and stormy make-believe.

Mrs. Cullen merely looked up at her husband and said in a velvety tone, "The trouble with Ireland, from my point of view, is that they don't like our having a falcon. Naturally Lord Bild disapproves; but I don't mind him. He's so unsure of himself; he's a Jew furthermore; you can scarcely expect him to live and let live. But our other neighbors and the family are almost as tiresome."

Cullen thrust the teasing hand in his pocket and returned to his armchair. Her eyes sparkled fast, perhaps with that form of contrition which pretends to be joking. Or perhaps it pleased her to break off the subject of their Irish circumstances and worldly situation and to resume the dear theme of hawk, which meant all the world to her.

The summer before, she told us, an old Hungarian

had sold her a trained tiercel. "I took him with me last winter when we stayed with some pleasant Americans in Scotland. There's a bad ailment called croaks, and he caught that and died. They had installed their American heating, which I think makes an old house damp; don't you? Then their gamekeeper trapped Lucy and gave her to me. Wasn't that lucky? I've always wanted a real falcon, a haggard, to man and train myself."

In strict terminology of the sport, she explained, only a female is called a falcon; and a haggard is one that has already hunted on her own account, that is, at least a year old when caught.

Except for that one deformed bit of one foot, Lucy was a perfect example of her species, *Falco peregrinus*, pilgrim hawk. Her body was as long as her mistress's arm; the wing feathers in repose a little too long, slung across her back like a folded tent. Her back was an indefinable hue of iron; only a slight patine of the ruddiness of youth still shone on it. Her luxurious breast was white, with little tabs or tassels of chestnut. Out of tasseled pantaloons her legs came down straight to the perch with no apparent flesh on them, enameled a greenish yellow.

But her chief beauty was that of expression. It was like a little flame; it caught and compelled your attention like that, although it did not flicker and there was

17

nothing bright about it nor any warmth in it. It is a look that men sometimes have; men of great energy, whose appetite or vocation has kept them absorbed every instant all their lives. They may be good men but they are often mistaken for evil men, and vice versa. In Lucy's case it appeared chiefly in her eyes, not black but funereally brown, and extravagantly large, set deep in her flattened head.

On each side of the upper beak there was a little tooth or tusk. Mrs. Cullen explained that the able bird in the prime of life uses this to snap the spinal cord of its quarry, which is the most merciful death in nature. It reminded me of the hooked gloves which our farmers wear to husk corn; and so in fact, I thought, it must work: the falcon in the sky like a large angelic hand, stripping the meat of pigeon or partridge out of its feathers, the soul out of its throat.

I think Mrs. Cullen was the most talkative woman I ever met; and it was hawk, hawk, all afternoon. A good many inhabitants of the British Isles are hell-bent all their lives upon killing some wild animal somehow, and naturally are keen about the domestic animals which assist them. Others, who know all about human nature, nevertheless prefer to converse about animals, perhaps because it is the better part of conversational valor. Mrs. Cullen's enthusiasm was nothing like that, and it probably would have annoyed or alarmed the majority of her compatriots. As it seemed to me after listening awhile, she felt welling up in her mind some peculiar imagination, or some trouble impossible to ignore, which she tried to relieve by talking, with a kind of continuous double meaning. I think she would never have admitted the duplicity, and perhaps could not have expressed herself in plain terms. People as a rule do mean much more than they understand.

She informed us, for example, that in a state of nature hawks rarely die of disease; they starve to death. Their eyesight fails; some of their flight feathers break off or fall out; and their talons get dull or broken. They cease to be able to judge what quarry is worth flying at; or their flight slows up so that even the likely quarry gets away. Or, because they have lost weight, the victim is not stunned by their swooping down on it. Or when they have clutched it, they cannot hang on long enough to kill. Day after day they make fools of themselves. Then they have to depend upon very young birds or sick birds, or little animals on the ground, which are the hardest of all to see; and in any case there are not enough of these easy conquests to keep them in flesh. The hungrier they get, the more wearily and weakly they hunt. And the weaker they get, the more often they go hungry, in a miserable confusion of cause and effect. Finally what appears to be shame and morbid discouragement overcomes them. They simply sit on the rocks or in a tree somewhere waiting to die, as you might say philosophically, letting themselves die.

"I met a man on the staff of our great madhouse in Dublin last year," Mrs. Cullen added. "I was curious to see what it was like; so he took me with him one afternoon on a tour of inspection. Some of the mad people reminded me of hawks, exactly." The lethargically mad, sitting with their hands in their laps, imaginarily exhausted, unable to speak above a whisper, with burning but unfocusable eyes, unable to concentrate . . .

Cullen cleared his throat boisterously, perhaps to protest against the curiosity of women or against this folly of reading meaning into the ways of mere birds.

Falconers believe that hunger must be worse for falcons than for other birds and animals, Mrs. Cullen said. It maddens them, with a soreness in every feather; an unrelievable itching in their awful feet; a bloody lump in their throats, with the light plumage wrapped loose around like a bandage. This painful greed, sick single-mindedness, makes it possible to tame them and to perfect the extraordinary technique of falconry, which is more than any other bird can learn. You hear it in their cry—*aik, aik*—as Mrs. Cullen then imitated it for us, ache, ache—a small flat scream with a bubbling or gargling undertone, as if their mouths were full of scalding water. "I suppose human beings never feel anything like it."

"But Madeleine, Madeleine, we're never hungry," her husband protested with a chuckle in which there was great satisfaction. "How can we tell?"

She begged him not to be silly. She had known people who had starved, Irish republicans hiding from the Black and Tans, Germans in 1922, and had inquired of them; and they had described it as rather a soft cool drowsy feeling.

I wondered about this. Although I had been a poor boy, on a Wisconsin farm and in a slum in Chicago and in Germany in 1922, I could not recollect any exact sensation of hunger, that is to say, hunger of the stomach. And I thought—as the relatively well-fed do think—of the other human hungers, mental and sentimental and so on. For example, my own undertaking in early manhood to be a literary artist. No one warned me that I really did not have talent enough. Therefore my hope of becoming a very good artist turned bitter, hot and nerve-racking; and it would get worse as I grew older. The unsuccessful artist also ends in an apathy, too proud and vexed to fly again, waiting upon with-held inspiration, bored to death . . . Naturally I did not speak of this to Alex and the Cullens. It seemed rude and somehow abnormal even to be thinking of it, while they sat exchanging information about real life, really starving nations and greedy species of bird.

Whereupon our present bird mantled, that is, stood a moment on one leg, shook the other leg and wing downward, and spread that half of her plumage in a long fan, gazing at me, blinking or winking at me. But because my writing had gone badly all spring I could not bear to give her more than a passing thought with reference to that. I began to think of her as an image of amorous desire instead. That is the great relief of weariness of work in any case; the natural consolation for its not going well. Or perhaps the Cullens' feeling about each other suggested it to me. No doubt art is too exceptional to be worth talking about; but sex is not. At least in good countries such as France and the United States during prosperous periods like the twenties, it must be the keenest of all appetites for a majority of men most of their lives.

And highly sexed men, unless they give in and get married and stay married, more or less starve to death. I myself was still young then and I had been lucky in love. But little early quarrels and failures warn one;

and in the confidences of friends and in gossip about other men, one discovers the vague beastly shape of what to expect. Life goes on and on after one's luck has run out. Youthfulness persists, alas, long after one has ceased to be young. Love-life goes on indefinitely, with less and less likelihood of being loved, less and less ability to love, and the stomach-ache of love still as sharp as ever. The old bachelor is like an old hawk.

Civilized human beings have learned how to avoid literal starvation and the fear of death and real enslavement; so at least it seemed in the twenties. They have this kind of thing instead: fear of old age, loss of charm, lack of love. Therefore I caught myself gazing at my young unmarried Alex anxiously, sentimentally, and at her Irish guests with idle envy. But the Irish wife's uneasiness and the husband's captivated but uncomfortable look reminded me that I was making a false distinction. There is not as much sweet safety in marriage as one hopes. Hunger and its twin, disgust, are in it too; need and greed; and passage of time, the punishment. Of course true love and lust are not the same, neither are they inseparable, nor indistinguishable. Only they reflect and imitate and elucidate each other.

Looking back upon that afternoon's talk and thought, I am inclined to hold Mrs. Cullen responsible for this daydreaming of mine, personal worry and ex-hilaration, which made me inattentive to what she said now and then. In a woman as energetic and at-tractive as that, the hint of hidden emotion and the sense of double meaning naturally are exciting; and the excitement leads in one's own private direction. But as it were in a mirror, looking at myself, I could see something of her character and plight before the cir-cumstances of the afternoon betrayed her. I think that was what she instinctively wanted.

Meanwhile she had gone on answering Alex's questions: something about the craftsmen who outfit falcons, generation after generation of avian haber-dashers especially in India, and which bell resounds the clearest through the grass and bushes and breezes, and what hood is least likely to ulcerate the waxen lids and lips; and something about an ancient Persian text with a thrice-hyphenated title which is still the best handbook of falconry. I wanted to know all this, yet I failed to pay attention.

Then Lucy bated, that is, threw herself headlong off the fist. The leather jesses around her legs and the leash looped through Mrs. Cullen's fingers held her ignominiously, upside down. It was a painful sight, like an epileptic fit or an insane fit. There was no possibility of the thongs breaking; I half-expected her lean bright legs to snap instead. I expected her to scream, aik! But the only sound was the jingling of her bell and the convulsion of her plumage, air panting through her plumage. The tail feathers and the flight feathers, shooting out rigidly, threshed against herself and against her mistress from head to foot. Mrs. Cullen, not the least disconcerted, raised her left arm straight up over her head, and stood up and stood quite still, only turning her face away from the flapping and whipping. Her equanimity impressed me as much as her strength.

In a minute Lucy gave up little by little. It was extraordinary: you could see her self-control returning, recurring in one feather after another. Then she hung peacefully like a mere turkey or goose hooked up in a butchershop; only for an instant. The long wings began again, but in a different exertion: hugging the air, bracing against the air, until her talons got a grip on the gauntlet and she succeeded in pulling herself up again where she belonged. There she stared or glared at us, blinking the rush of blood back out of her embarrassed eyes and pulling her plumage together.

With a sigh and a half-smile Mrs. Cullen brought her burdened and shaken arm down, and seated herself again in the straight chair. Some such hopeless attempt to escape, crazy fit of freedom, comes over all domesticated falcons at fairly regular intervals, she explained, especially in their first year or two; all their lives if they have not been well manned. "They never get over being wild. It's like malaria or that other intermittent fever, the one you have to be so careful about in the Orient."

Lucy happened to be an unusually frank, active bird, so that you could often tell when her trouble was to be expected; by a soft repeated tinkle of her bells or a steady pull at one of her jesses. The leather might of course be loose or worn out. "And instead it pinches her, which makes her angry, and everything seems hopeless," Mrs. Cullen concluded. "She can't help it, can't bear it. It's like committing suicide."

"Give me liberty or give me death, ha, ha," cried Cullen, seeming to expect special applause from us because we were Americans, or perhaps because Alex's name was Henry like the American who first expressed that sentiment. His wife gave him that look of hers which was the opposite of applause; and he took it as usual. His hazel eyes stood out like jewels; the tip of his tongue brightened his lips.

Meanwhile she was slowly caressing Lucy's lower plumage and tired feet. She might have been a trained nurse and Lucy her patient, after a bout of illness or craziness. Or she might have been in love and Lucy her beloved, pleasure absent-mindedly ebbing . . . And every word she uttered added a little to the confused significance. "Sometimes I can prevent her independent fits. The way a governess gets to know a child, and can see its tantrums beginning and distract it somehow . . . Being stroked like this often does the trick. At first I used a dried pigeon's wing as you're supposed to, but this suits Lucy as well."

Idly she went on with it: two dimpled fingers with long tinted nails and heavy rings just brushing the spent feathers. "Or if I notice it in time, I lift her over my head for a moment. She likes to perch as high as possible, so she can look down upon everything around her. I think it must frighten her to see things higher than she is. We're like that sometimes ourselves, aren't we?" she added, smiling gently.

Time after time her transitions like this—from hawk to human, objective to subjective—startled me. To be sure, any woman greatly in love must know how a flattery in time saves trouble, how the illusion of superiority counteracts the illusion of inferiority, as well as any governess. But it had not occurred to me that her love for Cullen was great in that sense: cunning, instructive, curative.

Falcons, she informed us, do not breed in captivity. Various attempts have been made to induce them to, but with no success. Thus, the entire sport has to start again from scratch for each falconer, whenever he trains a new playmate. Little by little the perfectly wild creature surrenders, individually, in the awful difficulty of hunger. But surrender is all, domestication is all; they never feel at home. You can carry male and female side by side on the same cadge year in and year out; nothing happens. They will cease to fight but they stay solitary. Scorn of each other for giving in, or self-scorn, seems to break their hearts. They never build a nest or lay an egg. Not one chick or eyas is ever reared in bondage. There is no real acceptance or inheritance of the state of surrender.

Mrs. Cullen mentioned, as a kind of exception, the make-hawks: old good-natured birds which some professionals use in the training of the young wild ones. But even their influence must be in the way of a rationalization of necessary evil, inculcation of vice, making the best of a bad bargain. For they too are born in the vacant rocks or uncomfortable trees; and they too keep sterile.

"Like schoolmasters," crowed Cullen. That appealed to my sense of humor. But Cullen's smile was a leer if I ever saw one, and evidently embarrassed his wife and Alex; so I kept from smiling.

Mrs. Cullen then quoted Buffon's famous sentence

about falcons: "*L'individu seul est esclave; l'espèce est libre.*" Buffon had been her father's second-best author, after Scott. Her French accent was incorrect but very pretty. Only the individual hawk is a slave; the species is free ...

Then Alex spoke up, in what was a loud voice for her: "Oh, dear, it is the opposite of human beings. We are slaves in the mass, aren't we? Only one man can hope to free himself; one at a time, then another, and another."

"Oh, I dare say," Mrs. Cullen assented. "Yes, perhaps." But she smiled patronizingly. I think she was congratulating herself upon knowing a freer and stronger type of humanity than our pampered, subtle, self-questioning American type; and perhaps she did: Irish republicans, wild Hungarians with hawks, Germans during their defeat.

"But it is true, isn't it?" Alex insisted. "The man who really loves freedom is the exception."

"Oh, quite. How right you are," our lady falconer dubiously murmured.

But her husband disagreed. "No, Alex! What a disgusting idea! Love of liberty is the deepest instinct we have—if you will excuse my saying so."

We silently considered this for a moment; the three of us, it seemed, regretfully. Alex wanted freedom more than anything; and if others as a rule did not, she might have a lonely life. In any case it would take a better man than Cullen to dispel her young misanthropy. I myself regretted never having been able to decide what to think: how much liberty is a true human motive, and how much is wasteful and foolish? And for the first time that afternoon Mrs. Cullen gazed at her husband sadly, that is, weakly. She agreed with him, I felt sure. But there are circumstances in which it may be obvious that at least one human being requires freedom; and you bitterly regret that it is so: because you need to keep that one captive.

"Why, hang it all," Cullen still sputtered, "why, independence is the only thing that is human about hawks. Don't you agree, Madeleine?"

She slightly turned her back to him and contemplated Alex and me rather unkindly. It was the careful absence of expression, absence of frown, that you see on a clever lecturer's face when the irrelevant questioning or heckling begins. There was also a sadness about it which, if I read it aright, I have often felt myself. She did not want us to take her hawk, her dear subject-matter, her hobby and symbol—whatever it meant to her—and turn it this way and that to mean what we liked. It was hers and we were spoiling it. Around her eyes and mouth there were lines of that caricatural weariness which is peculiar to those who talk too much.

Indeed our sociability as a whole had gone off; something a little sour and dark had developed in it. We had been sitting there too long. Alex, I fancied, was counting the minutes until they departed. But suddenly she grew hospitable. "You'll stay to dinner, Madeleine, won't you? Please, Larry, do. I can promise you a good dinner," she added with an indulgent smile.

I wondered whether she had mentioned this invitation to Jean and Eva, and whether the short notice would exasperate or inspire them. Mrs. Cullen also thought of that. "Servants are devils, don't you know. Mine used to behave madly, when extra people turned up at Cullen Hall."

Poor Alex was accustomed to the madness of servants; but, as she explained, this new couple did not mind surprises. She had found them in Tangier, where the secretary of the pig-sticking club had engaged them to cook in camp for several tentfuls of unmarried members. With only primitive utensils, a few iron kettles and a spit over an outdoor fire, and unpredictable guests at all hours, it evidently was child's play for them, and a welcome opportunity to show off. One afternoon a French general and a party of eight had motored out from the town, and some thoughtless fellow had asked

31

them to stay. Jean had taken a boar killed that morning, and by slicing it thin, rubbing it with certain herbs which grew there underfoot amid the tents, and marinating it in four bottles of brandy, rendered it quite edible by nightfall. Alex was inclined to think of her entire lifetime as an emergency of that sort. So she had hired the proud pair and secured passports for them and embarked them for France and Chancellet. And this, she told Mrs. Cullen, was what she had hired them for.

"If we do stay," Mrs. Cullen said, "my bird will have to be fed, toward six o'clock." Alex in any case intended to suggest to Jean a dish of pigeons baked with white currants. He would procure them from a neighbor who had an immense old dovecot; and one could be brought back alive for Lucy. The reminiscence of the brandied wild pig, the prospect of *pigeons aux groseilles*, charmed Cullen; you could see the gourmandise shining on his rosy lips.

Alex went to the kitchen, and by her comfortable air when she came back I judged that Jean was well disposed. Then she suggested our taking a walk until dinner-time, which also charmed Cullen, though his appetite did not need whetting. "By Jove," he said, "I do look forward to those squabs."

They were disappointed to learn that the park was

not Alex's property. It belonged to the nation, along with the little château de Chancellet in the midst of it. Bidou, the illustrious aged ex-minister, was permitted to live there. But he kept the gates open in the daytime, and the entire village strolled in and out. Meeting all classes when he took his daily exercise perhaps made him think proudly how democratic a statesman he had been all his life. He gave everyone a *bonjour*. He especially liked meeting Alex because she was an American and he vaguely remembered having advocated the payment of the war debts.

"Oh, aren't politicians a bore?" Cullen exclaimed with an odd proud laugh. "Worse than poets."

"Larry, please," his wife said in haste, "please let's not talk about that." I wondered what that meant.

Alex unlocked the little gate on the far side of the pond, and we strolled along an *allée* of ancient beeches. She warned us that if Bidou should appear in the distance, she would have to turn back. He had a way of inviting her to dine, and Mme. Bidou had asked her not to accept on account of the failing of his health, the folly of his old manhood.

We all felt happier now that we were outdoors. It was beautiful in the park. The trees had been so lovingly tended ever since a pupil of Lenôtre's set them out that each had developed its maximum character.

The way they stood in informal groups, or in line, or alone at a little distance, seemed not only to conform to the art of parks but to express their feelings about each other: idiosyncrasies of affection or obedience, pride or pain. And unlike human characters in such an assembly, they promised or threatened nothing more; no episodes or developments.

Cullen walked up ahead with Alex. Now in the open air he not only laughed but shouted; so that I could hear him telling her a yarn about an old English politician who had attached himself to a young married woman. And one day he and the husband had gone out alone together on the moor for a bit of rough shooting; and he had shot the husband by accident, so to speak. Then he had married her. But he had worried about it all the rest of his life, which was not long; and he had impoverished her in his will. It was ancient gossip: I had heard it before; and at the time I did not see any oddity in Cullen's telling it, except that it seemed funny to him and not to me. When love is diabolic, I thought, a triangle is the simplest form it can take; and a convenient form, if it cannot be endured. The lovers to be pitied perhaps are those who have no one to hate—what they long to kill, and what the killing would be for, incorporated in one and the same person, the one they love—whose rough shooting therefore can take place only in imagination, and never ends.

Presently we came to a crossroads; and there we did see the short silhouette of old Bidou headed in our direction: his peculiar march or trudge, and the shrugging of his shoulders inside a great cape. All his life he had gone booted like a common soldier and blackly wrapped up, which had been a boon to caricaturists and a kind of electoral trade mark; which now made it easy to avoid him. Mrs. Cullen asked if they might go on ahead and have a look at the famous old fellow.

Alex and I turned back alone toward her house, by a short cut through a dense plantation of young trees, with vernal branches of old trees rounded overhead. It was like walking inside a great recumbent telescope, pointed at the château half a kilometer away. In the nineteenth century, under the personal supervision of Viollet-le-Duc and his friend the author of *Carmen*, Chancellet had been entirely and fussily restored. In the round bit of sunshine afar off, the lens of our telescope, it looked too good to be true, amid the patchy flower beds and the moat, where a few ducks were splashing and lovemaking.

I was in as foolish a good humor as Cullen; everything seemed mysterious and sentimental. The rounded frame of branches in which we strolled, looking ahead into pinkish sunlight; the tidy little architecture enframed, with its associations literary as well as historical; the dying, absent-minded, erotic statesman exercising daily in an immutable circle around it; our odd guests walking to meet him, woman with hawk and greedy man, whose eyes turned golden when he looked at her, whose spit ran at the mere mention of his dinner—all were gathered around me, I vainly fancied, to make one great vague thing very simple and clear to me. What more could I ask? But it is always foolish to expect simplicity. All one can do is to substitute little facts for great speculations, little performances for immense desire, and call this, simplification.

The return by ourselves gave me a chance to question Alex about the Cullens. They had come to Tangier two or three years before for the pig-sticking. Madeleine rode ideally, but the rule of the club forebade women to carry a spear. Cullen had shown a definite lack of enthusiasm and indeed a lack of talent; however, he had gone out every day and not done badly. When one of the vile brave beasts appeared in the distance—flickering along the shrub, suddenly fleeing out across open ground like the shadow of a flying bird—the Irishwoman would gallop out with the very first riders; her husband following hard, looking as if he might fall any minute but not falling. At the last minute, when the spears began to point down along the shoulders of the horses, she would rein up short or turn aside. Suddenly she would not be there any longer, and Cullen still would be. Her ambition for him and his poor horsemanship—so it appeared to the others—betrayed him into prowess. Alex heard a club member say that once or twice at the kill his audacity and ferocity had been rather too much of a good thing; shocking. One morning his horse stepped into a hole and threw him right down beside the boar, a big wicked one already wounded; and he behaved with great sense and courage, and kept his horse away from its tushes, although he was not quite sober. His not being quite sober was the trouble in general.

One afternoon Mrs. Cullen had said as much to Alex. "Poor Larry, when we're in Ireland or in London with nothing to do, is inclined to overeat, and furthermore to drink far too much." Alex must have been impressed by this confession, for she quoted some of it word for word. "Most things are a beastly bore for him, you know; that's his real weakness. But you can't say anything to a grown man about drinking, after all, can you? It's such a horrid little unimportant thing. They're proud, and they resent having to think of it. I had an aunt who talked about it, and it made my uncle worse." As discreetly as she could therefore, she told Alex, she tried to keep him distracted; busy doing things, in good company which inspired him to do well; abroad, and outdoors as much as possible. He often complained that it was no way to live; but it had kept him fit and good-natured.

She was younger than he, Alex pointed out; and she had money of her own; and she was a clever, unconventional, and rather self-indulgent woman. Yet she devoted herself entirely to him, every instant, year in and year out. He on the other hand was not perfectly faithful, in spite of his devotion to her. When they were in Tangier a pretty young American named Baroness Levene came across from Malaga, and flirted with Cullen; and he obviously responded to it. One of the Tangier residents asked them all to dine, and while the men stayed in the dining room, Madeleine had been very rude to the little interloper. A day or two later she spoke of it apologetically. It was disgraceful of her, she assured Alex, to mind her husband's virile frivolity. She never doubted for an instant that he loved her, and no other woman. His response to the others was all make-believe or in fun. She alluded again to his deadly tedium; his need of some novelty to pass the time somehow, every day of his life, every hour; and his other weaknesses in direct consequence. A little philandering, like eating and drinking, gave him something to think about.

Whereas marriage was infinitely simple for her, she said; she never needed the attention of other men. She supposed this to be so settled and so apparent in her character that it bored men and they let her alone. Alex had observed a number of acceptable men not letting her alone in the least; rather smitten. Yet there seemed to be no affectation or insincerity in Mrs. Cullen's account of herself. Women who have been spoiled by the many, tormented by one, often have an air of innocence.

Alex had seen a great deal of them the following winter in London; and there they were engaged in a very odd sport indeed: underground activity of Irish rebellion. Cullen was perfectly and anciently Irish, and one of his brothers had been a friend of Casement's. Whereas Madeleine was not a Catholic; and she had Ulster blood and English blood; and as a child she had lived in Canada. Yet she was the rebel, or she ardently played the part of one; Larry followed. Alex heard him speak very angrily of the British, disgustedly of de Valera. But he loved joining in others' opinion, no matter what, and embellishing his repetition of it, as best he could—how could one tell what he thought? Perhaps it was hard for him to tell himself.

All that winter they were at home informally almost every evening to the oddest patriots. At first glance it looked like a literary salon. The ringleader was the poet McVoy: a young man of great conversation, with a half-rapacious, half-religious face. Alex also met a man who had done a little bombing, another with a bit of his cheek shot away, and certain bereaved and cruel women, and a bizarre priest. Their political opinion was all tinged with piety, even puritanism. They would have been ashamed to eat or drink or be merry in any way, with so much to be done for Eire. Cullen yielded to the general austerity. Furthermore, he told Alex, they could not afford to live well that winter, because of their contributions to the cause. Alex had never seen him in better form, lean and youthful and, if not exactly cheerful, amiable. Rebellion evidently served as an excellent exercise and diet. There was also amorous anxiety: he thought McVoy in love with Madeleine. Alex indeed thought so too. But all Madeleine appeared to want of the poet was to keep on his political high horse, in his fascinating conspiratorial vein, for Larry's amusement. Rioting and sabotage and perhaps even assassination—as it were sticking of the Ulster pig, mort of the English stag—with poor Larry in the thick of it, because it would be good for him ... Suddenly all that ceased, Alex never heard why. They sublet their house and spent the summer in Vienna and Budapest. That was the summer Mrs. Cullen bought her first hawk, the tiercel that died of the croaks.

This little information Alex gave me as we sauntered slowly through the ex-minister's park. Now we were back near our gate, under the great beeches. Alex had been a little anxious lest the Cullens get lost. But there in the broken light, pallid shade, there they came at a brisk pace, engaged in a vivacious discussion of some sort, which they ceased as soon as they saw us. "He's a dear, your old politician," Mrs. Cullen said. "He spoke to us, and then what do you suppose he did? He did bird imitations for Lucy; I mean to say, he whistled at her."

Evidently Cullen preferred French politicians to Irish. "A good old boy! He did a nightingale and a lark and some bird I didn't know. He told us what it was, but it was French. Quite good."

"And Larry, wasn't he cheerful and civil? Perhaps he thought that if he kept whistling long enough, Lucy would answer. Wasn't it funny?"

I thought it touching as well as funny: that old man had been whistling to his compatriots like that for half a century, and as a rule a majority had answered; but, alas, nothing much had come of it, for France.

Now Mrs. Cullen was ready to feed Lucy. But her chauffeur and Jean, who had gone to the neighbor's dovecot, had not returned. Foolish Eva felt sure they were in a ditch somewhere, or quarreling, or lost. So we sat down again; and I like a fool inquired what they thought of French and English and German politics. Cullen was out of breath but he sniffed wonderfully and cleared his throat, preliminary to an opinion. "Please, Larry, no politics," his wife requested, smiling at me to make it less impolite.

She was fondling Lucy, gazing at her eye to eye, slowly shaking her head at her; and the wicked beak moved in exact obedience to the tip of her nose as if it were magnetized. "Lucy's hungry," she said solemnly.

"Feel her breast." She took my hand and held it against the tasseled plumage; and indeed there was a humming and stiffening in it, like a little voltage of electricity. Her eyes were moist and explosive; and the instant her mistress's eyes released them, down they went to the gauntlet, as if expecting a feathery form in agony to materialize out of the leather.

"Feel her feet," Mrs. Cullen added; and I did, while she explained that birds always have a higher temperature than animals. Fever heat; and yet they were slick and dry like a serpent. I could feel what they wanted to do, what they wanted to have, swelling in them and ticking the dull minutes meanwhile with little throbs. My pleasure in touching them was half embarrassment; and it set my mind running back to the thought I had left off an hour ago; that this hawk's hunger was like amorous appetite. I call it thought—and it is thought now, as I remember and try to tell it—but at the time it was only a vague flashing daydream. It all came together like one large composite phrase: old bachelor hungry bird, aging-hungry-man-bird, and how I hate desire, how I need pleasure, how I adore love, how difficult middle age must be!

Then, I lamented to myself, if your judgment is poor you fall in love with those who could not possibly love you. If romance of the past has done you any harm, you will not be able to hold on to love when you do attain it; your grasp of it will be out of alignment. Or pity or self-pity may have blunted your hand so that it makes no mark. Back you fly to your perch, ashamed as well as frustrated. Life is almost all perch. There is no nest; and no one is with you, on exactly the same rock or out on the same limb. The circumstances of passion are all too petty to be companionable. So there you sit, and you try to sit still, and doze and dream to save trouble. It is the kind of thing you have to keep quiet about for others' sake, politeness's sake: itching palm and ugly tongue and unsighted eye and empty flatulent physiology as a whole; and your cry of desire, ache, ache, ringing in your own ears. No one else hears it; and you get so tired of it yourself that you can't wait to grow old . . .

Thus in an instant I foolishly imagined myself growing old; and meanwhile Mrs. Cullen had not ceased speaking with that single-minded vivacity of hers, but a little somber. "Since we caught Lucy," she said, "she's never had a mouthful to eat except out of my hand, and I've always worn the same glove. Think what it must mean to her!"

It was an impressive unpleasant object, that glove, stiffened and discolored by a hundred little sanguinary banquets. It resembled things you see in cases in anthropological museums; fetishes of awful religion, sacrificial utensils, witch-doctors' kits. And the feet with crescent toenails trod it so passionately that you wondered how the wrist inside endured it.

"You know, she's not really attached to me personally," Mrs. Cullen said. "If I gave you the glove she'd be yours instead of mine. It's as simple as that, I think. It's what's called behaviorism, isn't it? Would you like to try it? Try taking her a moment."

She turned around and held Lucy some five or six inches below the chair-back, and after a moment's hesitation Lucy hopped up there. Mrs. Cullen's hand was large and mine is not; so that I was able to squeeze into the gauntlet. It surprised me to see that she wore another large diamond on that hand, which under the pressure of the leather had bruised her finger a little . . . Then I held my wrist five or six inches above the chair-back; and Lucy, with her belief in food-stained leather added to her belief in the highest possible perch, hopped again.

"That's what they call an inferiority complex, don't they?" Cullen proudly demanded, not to be outdone by his wife's use of that other catchword. "Madeleine can't understand one thing about psychology."

"Very well, Larry. I tell you she's hungry," his wife answered. And by the tone of her voice you would have thought her the hungry one.

I drew a deep breath, in which I got the hawk odor, slightly bloody, slightly peppery. I had noticed it before, but without distinguishing it from Mrs. Cullen's French scent. The body, well balanced on its hot feet, weighed less than I had supposed. At the least move her talons pricked the leather and pulled it a bit—as fashionable women's fingernails do on certain fabrics —though evidently she held them as loose and harmless as she could. Only her grip as a whole was hard, like a pair of tight, heated iron bracelets.

Alex offered her congratulations upon Lucy's

evident peace of mind with me; I would make a good falconer. That reminded me of my father and his magic with animals which filled me with envy and antipathy when I was a boy. He could force a crazy colt to its knees, or castrate a young boar, or chloroform a desperate trapped owl; and their wretched muscles relaxed and surrendered, their eyes blinked in perfect gentleness in alignment with his eyes. His eyes, or perhaps it was his hands, seemed able to promise them something. Half my life, I said to myself, has been discovering that my character is not the antithesis or the contradiction of his; here was a new kinship. Perhaps I could cope with horse or hog or doomed bird too, if I had to; perhaps even with a wild antipathetic son, disinclined to live—who knows? This was a gratifying thought but not altogether happy: vast vague potentiality of things I did not wish to do in any case.

I happen to be a trifle long-sighted; and now Lucy was so close that I could not quite see her in focus; and I have always had a fear of going blind. One good flutter, one simple thrust, and she could have slit an eyelid or ruptured an eyeball in an instant. She did not shuffle much on the borrowed gauntlet. But the vague dilated dark of her eye, the naked ring around it, the inner eyelids opening and closing as instantly as bubbles, seemed worse than restlessness. I was ashamed to tell her mistress that I was afraid. No doubt the chances of her actually hurting me were negligible. Mrs. Cullen's half-supercilious glance at us was reassuring. Still, I felt rather as if I had a great thought of death concentrated and embodied and perched on me. Whatever had possessed me, I wondered, to think of this Lucy—bloodthirsty brute with a face like a gouge, feet like two sets of dirty scalpels—as significant of love? Perhaps those two things, imaginary death and hopeless desire, always lie close together in one's mind, foolishly interchangeable.

Mrs. Cullen meanwhile, with vacated wrist, seemed the most restless woman in the world. She kept crossing and uncrossing her perfect stilted feet; leaning this way and that in the soft armchair; clasping and unclasping her jeweled fingers. It suggested one more explanation of her attachment to Lucy; falconry made her sit still. Perhaps too she was slightly jealous of my successful deputyship. "The real reason Lucy likes you so much," she murmured, "is that it's getting on toward mealtime. She fancies you may have a little steak or half a pigeon in your pocket. You look promising to her. What do you suppose has become of your cook? I do hope he and Ricketts haven't gone off to get drunk together."

She rose and tripped across to the great window. She

tripped back and paused beside us and teased Lucy as Cullen had done, but in the opposite spirit. The star sapphire slid a little from one teasing finger to the next, which Lucy observed with interest. It looked like an unsocketed eye, I thought.

"Oh, Alex," Mrs. Cullen said, "you're so intelligent. I'm afraid you think me very sentimental. I'm not really. I do not want a falcon to be attached to me personally. When animals get that sort of feeling, it's too awful. Knowing the sound of your voice, liking the way you smell, wanting to be touched, all that. I hate it. It's such a parody of us, it's worse than we are. A bird like Lucy is so simple and straight. You make a promise and she expects you to keep it, that's all. She knows what she wants, and who gives it to her, and that's that."

Cullen grunted, and assured us that his wife didn't mean a word of this cynical stuff. But he did agree about one thing: "Birds are selfish as the devil. That's why I can't care for them. I'd rather have a dog, I tell you."

"Do you hear, Lucy? He'd rather have a dog." She said this in the way of wicked affectation, perhaps toying with the idea of being hated by him for it.

Then she turned briskly to me: "I'll take her back now, Mr. Tower, if you please. I think she'll bate in a minute."

Once more we exchanged the glove. Once more Lucy considered, on the rough leather, the stain of yesterday's meals and the hope of today's and tomorrow's, and leaped up with alacrity. Her mistress carefully fondled her to prevent her bating, but she bated nevertheless.

After that, Mrs. Cullen heaved a greater sigh than before, not because it had been a harder struggle, but because her own light but significant remarks had hurt her at last, I fancied. And now she added that, simple though hawks all were, you could never really trust one. "Oh, I shall have to be so careful, never to fly Lucy at things she cannot catch and kill. The least failure makes her hopeless. My man in Hungary says that if she misses her quarry twice, I must call it a day and keep her hooded; otherwise it's risky. Because if she should miss a third time she might leave me; fly off and never return. They're all alike: the haggard you've hunted with for years; even the eyas you have taken from the nest and babied all its life . . ."

"Damned ungrateful, I say," Cullen jeered.

"No, Larry. Lucy gives up her freedom and stays with me because it's a better life, more food and more fun. If it doesn't work, after all, what's the use? If my falconry isn't good enough . . ."

Cullen giggled. I didn't. For it is the way religious

49

faith goes, in the sense of God's failure; and it is the way true love ends: missing the third time. That much of life I already knew; I had missed twice. I glanced at Alex, wondering if the mysterious turn this small talk was taking troubled her too. But her face had its pretty well-bred passivity; I could not tell. The light in the Irishwoman's eyes was fantastic, focused like glass on her great weak husband, then on me for just a moment with something like embarrassing affection. She and I understood each other.

She seemed to me a very passionate woman, but it was a kind of plural passion, all confused or crossed: work and play and sense of beauty, the maternal and the conjugal and the misanthropic, mixed. Perhaps that is a peculiarity of childless women. Female character has a great many secondary traits and minor talents; the wear and tear of motherhood may weaken them or stamp them out. It is anarchy if they all flourish.

"Tower," she said, "you would make a good falconer. Why don't you take it up, in the States? And you too, Alex. Everyone should have some hobby, some pet, I think. And all the other pets really are too awful.

"Ugh, how I despise dogs!" she then exclaimed in a dull disgusted tone of voice. "Do you know what dogs remind me of? It's not a nice thing to say but I do mean it. Prostitutes; all things to all men, and all that.

And all shapes and sizes, from adapting themselves to everything and everybody for centuries, with no integrity. Men love them for that; it's flattering.

"Falcons have never changed. Forty centuries of falconry, think of it! And still wild; every feather as it was, and the same everywhere. I tell you, there's nothing like it in nature. Cats have more character than dogs, if they only weren't so damned amorous. Kittens to be drowned every few months, isn't it awful!"

My well-bred Alex in spite of herself made a little shocked face. It startled me too, because just then like a fool I had been thinking of Mrs. Cullen as a childless woman. What about those wild Irish sons of hers, shifting for themselves at Cullen Hall, riding and spoiling her favorite hunters, hunting with Lord Bild? I said a kind of prayer for them. That is, I hoped that they really were wild. Cullen had spoken of them as practically mature men; but perhaps he himself was not mature enough to judge of it. I hoped that they did not love their mother much. If they were at all backward or sensitive it was good of her, wise of her, to keep out of Ireland.

At this point wild Lucy flung up her wings and let her mute drop to the floor. Mrs. Cullen cheerfully apologized, and also proudly called our attention to its whiteness. It meant that Lucy was in excellent health.

A healthy falcon's mute is the cleanest wastage in nature, and by no stretch of imagination could Alex or I have been offended by it. Cullen offendedly stirred his great body about in the great soft armchair; his face got redder; his light eyes protruded. But they protruded at us rather than it. Perhaps he feared, or perhaps hoped, that we would somehow express disapprobation or disgust. Alex rang for Eva, and of course that simple creature did not mind; it rather amused her. She fetched a towel and some wax, and knelt beautifully, and gave the parquet a very good restoration.

During which, Jean came rushing in, sweaty and pleased with himself. When he saw his dear beauty there on her knees he made a gleeful sound and gave her a tap as he passed, which made her blush. He and Ricketts in the Daimler had had a blowout on the back road. But dinner would not be much delayed; for while Ricketts had changed the tire, he had seated himself by the roadside and dressed the pigeons with his jackknife.

Mrs. Cullen asked him how large Lucy's pigeon was; and he sent Eva after it: a rumpled thing in a basket with warm damned eyes. She instructed them to wring its neck and chop it in half and bring it back, with its feathers and half the giblets. Meanwhile she asked me to move the straight chair into a dusky corner under the staircase. Though the least shy hawk in the world, Lucy would not feed properly outdoors or with a light in her eyes. Next Mrs. Cullen requested a number of towels to protect her dress, and Eva brought a worn-out tablecloth; and Alex helped tie this under her chin like a bib and spread it out over her lap. She sat with her pretty legs far apart, no longer a fashionable woman but rather like a gypsy or a priestess; or as if this were to be some surgical operation or painful travail.

Whereupon Jean returned with the portion of pigeon. He let two or three drops of blood and a bit of gizzard fall on the waxed floor; and again Eva cheerfully mopped up. Mrs. Cullen took the half-bird in the hand on which Lucy perched, pinching it between gloved forefinger and thumb, at Lucy's feet; turning it temptingly. At first Lucy stared at Alex and me so insolently that we drew a few steps away from the staircase. Jean and Eva also wanted to watch, but Alex reminded them that we too were hungry.

I had been hearing so much and thinking so romantically of hawk-hunger that I expected a lunge and a grab, like a wolf or a cat; it was not so at all. It took two or three minutes for Lucy's appetite to develop, to accumulate. In a state of nature, no doubt it depends upon the fun of pursuit, voluptuous air in her wings, and the hovering and teasing; and there would not be any real spasm of Lucy's love of food until the instant she felt food in her beak. Now there had to be time for some equivalent of all that to take place in her narrow mind; time at least to regret it. The tedium of this conjugal kind of repast had to be overcome somehow; so she doubted and deliberated and imagined.

"Damn your pride, Lucy," Mrs. Cullen muttered; then murmured to us in her schoolgirl French, because Lucy did not understand French, "*L'appétit vient en mangeant.*" Upon which I reminded myself that on the whole, throughout life as a whole, the appetites which do not arise until we have resolved to eat, which we cannot comprehend until we have eaten, are the noblest—marital, aesthetic, religious . . .

At last Lucy's curly breast did throb; a few feathers bristled up; her wings stood out a few inches; her greenish fists clenched on the glove; then her whole body began to point down beak first like a water-diviner's stick. She set her feet a little farther apart on her mistress's wrist. Then she stooped straight between them and thrust into the piece of pigeon. Mrs. Cullen held it tight. Lucy braced her legs and pulled and straightened back up with a morsel, which after a moment she shifted away into her throat and, with a sinuous motion or a toss, swallowed.

Until the end, until there was no more pigeon, Mrs. Cullen had to encourage her to keep her mind on what she was doing. "The important thing," she said, "is to get her to take feathers enough. Her digestion depends a good deal on that."

When Lucy paused and raised her weird face between mouthfuls, it seemed spiritual rather than sensual; a bigoted face. There was no histrionic angry temper, no showing off. Thoroughly and slowly it went on to the end, with meditation upon every feather, every crumb of meat, every sip of blood—sacramental. Once or twice, because she did not like the way some wisp of plumage or tiny tendon felt—or because she liked it extremely—she shook her head hard; and a spot of blood appeared on Mrs. Cullen's bib, a feather drifted to the floor. Perhaps you could not have watched it if you were squeamish; neither Alex nor I were. But after the fourth or fifth beakful Lucy had a bad moment, modesty or imaginary repletion, and Mrs. Cullen asked us to move still farther away; and we were glad to go. We sat down beside Cullen in front of the big window.

It interested me to observe, or to guess at, his feeling about this. When his wife first called for Lucy's banquet he had pulled a long face. I think that may have been only fond anxiety, lest in her serving of it she appear to Alex and me coarse, or comical. He kept his eyes averted, but it was not disgust, surely, for it put him in mind of his own eating. He talked to us of that with enthusiasm and in great detail. In Paris the past week someone had sent them away out on the Avenue Jean Jaurès for a steak; year after year they always telephoned a certain small unsuccessful restaurant to prepare a supreme *cassoulet* which took two days; and so forth. Which brought him finally to the present, the great casserole of pigeons which Jean was preparing. At that point, I think, Alex regarded him almost with detestation.

The half-pigeon out of the way, Mrs. Cullen decided to put Lucy outdoors to weather, as it is called. We followed her into the garden where she selected the back of a rustic bench as a suitable perch. But there had been signs of more than usual nervousness during the feeding: it seemed best to leave her hooded. Because of the unaccustomed warmth of the afternoon, after Scotland, Mrs. Cullen said, she had a slight headache; and she retired with Alex to the bedroom for some aspirin and a moment's repose.

Then I offered Cullen a cocktail. He rose with enthusiasm and followed me to what I called the choir loft, that is, the balcony, where Alex's decorator had seen fit to install a bar, in the fashion of the twenties:

all chromium and copper with a fine hierarchy of glasses and remarkable liquors in odd bottles. My Irishman had never seen the like of it. There was a magnum of prewar vodka; and I suggested a kind of modified Alexander with that in it instead of gin. Missing a syllable, he thought it charming of me, and so American, to serve a drink named after our hostess. I tried to set him right on that point but he was too charmed to care. The drink itself also suited him and for a while he concentrated on it, without a word.

The ladies did not return, so presently I mixed a second shakerful; and Alex's silver shaker was large. It was indiscreet, perhaps a little perverse, and in a way characteristic of me. As a rule I dislike being with people who have had too much to drink. It often brings on in me a kind of misanthropic fit: pity verging upon repugnance, and a mean sense of humor which they sometimes notice. But just because I am aware of the old-maidishness and even injustice of this, whenever the hospitality of the bottle is up to me I am inclined to overdo it.

Cullen in fact had been a little tight all afternoon, and I had not realized it. Now as he got tighter I saw that it was the same thing. They had arrived at Chancellet about two-thirty; so probably it had happened at luncheon, perhaps at breakfast. That explained his wife's anxious and resentful air, and her rude motherly snubs to keep him in order. He must have been in misery the last few hours, while we failed to offer him anything: thoughtlessness on my part, perhaps prudence or dislike on Alex's. She of course knew him well and must have noticed.

Perhaps the unnoticeable sort of heavy daytime drinker has the worst trouble; certainly they are more troublesome to others than they think. And others— sobersides like myself—are often more unjust to them than to their reeling, roaring, festive confreres. Half the time they themselves are only half aware of any incapacity or lack of charm. Or perhaps they know, and they think that you do not, and you do, and of course it is not manners to tell them so. They make an effort, often a heroic effort; and you feel that you have to respect and applaud that, whether or not it is fun for you.

But the worst injustice must be when you scarcely know them, and you judge them without reference to their habit, as in my case with Cullen that afternoon. He had simply seemed to me mediocre; old for his age, and weak for his size, dull, vain, and rather cross. No one had warned me that I was not seeing him at his best. It was his character, for all I knew, the nature of the creature; take it or leave it. That is to say, I had left it. So now I felt a slight embarrassment and grudging contrition.

Perhaps at other times, I reminded myself, his character was ideal; his mind vigorous; his great physique fresh and energetic. That would explain the love his wife bore him. Suppose you have learned to like or to love such a man when he was sober; and you happen to dislike him when he is not; and he doesn't know the difference or can't help it. The temptation to interfere, the fond hope of reformation, must be very great. Thus I began to think indulgently of Mrs. Cullen's selfish nervousness and sharp tongue. Although, if what I had seen that afternoon was the worst of it, certainly she exaggerated and overemphasized the plight she was in with him. An ordinary boring conceited uneasy childish man! Yet out of his petty instability she seemed to expect something odious or dangerous to develop any minute—as if she felt the ground underfoot move a bit, like a landslide starting, and caught glimpses of little creeping sickening things close to the surface, coming up! Love itself is an exaggeration, and very likely to lead to others.

After the first pouring of the second round, suddenly Cullen began a long complaint of the merry chase she led him year in and year out: her Mediterranean cruises, her falcons, her Irish republicans.

No home to speak of, no creature comforts; nothing like the good time Alex and I had here in Chancellet, this pretty bar for example. Nothing but wild men, wild birds, and two silly maids to mop up after the birds instead of a good cook: hotel food all the year round, never a leg of boar soaked in brandy or squab with currants.

At first, I think his outburst embarrassed him as well as me. For he explained that if I were an Englishman he would not be talking to me in this way; nor, for that matter, if he were an Englishman! But the Irish are like Americans in this respect. He had been in the States three or four years when he was a young fellow; therefore he felt the likeness. "The English never talk freely, as we're talking now. They're sly; they simply rule, and have their own way about everything. Britannia rules the waves and so on. You know, Tower, my wife's English . . ."

These little distinctions of nationality were what reminded him of their winter in London with the Irish republicans. He not only disliked that type of Irish; their political principle seemed suspect to him. "They're not really republicans, that's just talk. They're anarchists. It was beastly for me. I'm a fool, I'd do anything in the world for my wife, and she does whatever strikes her fancy. She kept asking those patriots to the house. It cost me a pretty penny too, I can tell you. I had to pay for a lot of pamphlets, I had to support two widows, I had to hire halls for their meetings. Then, if you please, some of 'em said they needed some guns and bombs. Can you believe it? Only I don't think they got any bombs. Nothing happened. It would serve the English right if they did blow things up, you know. I suppose my wife's little friends just pocketed the money; or they bought a poor make of bomb that wouldn't do. Nothing happened."

He also complained that they were comic little characters, not gentlemen. And all their women appeared half-crazed with loving them, weeping in the corridor, losing their tempers with each other; some of them occult, some religious, and all of course talking Ireland, Ireland. Not a class of women that a man of a sensual nature would look twice at, not if he had any self-respect; nothing soft or sweet or tidy about them. "But I must say I enjoyed it for a while," he admitted, "seeing how that class of people get on and hearing their stories. I could always shut them up when I felt like it, or chuck them all altogether, you understand, because I had the money."

Of course I had begun to feel my misanthropy; but still his monologue amused me, especially the vulgar touches like this last. No doubt he was a quite good county aristocrat of that modest rank which as a rule is less mixed than any other. But not even aristocracy can be expected to give good examples of itself all the time. It seems rather to secrete commonness little by little, and to keep it in reserve, along with those odds and ends of mere human nature which aristocratic manners are intended to hide. And every generation or two it purges itself, in the form of some odd son or daughter, perfect little shopkeeper or predestined courtesan, upon whom manners wear thin.

Cullen silently ruminated two or three minutes; and when he began again it was in the middle of a new bit of subject matter. Probably it seemed to him that he had told me something which he had been saying to himself, something about his wife. "Make no mistake, Tower, I respect my wife." And he went on to assure me, or to warn me, that anyone who doubted it or slighted her in the least was quite likely to be knocked down by him; in fact he had done it once. She was like a swan in his opinion; pure as snow, with never a harmful thought all her life. "Only she's thoughtless," he added. "She never thinks of anything except what she happens to want. She's spoiled. When I met her she was the prettiest girl in Dublin. Lovely breasts for one thing. And ankles; you saw her ankles! Her family wasn't well off either; I took her without a penny; and I've spoiled her."

Aristocracy had nothing to do with it. It was my own fault; the vodka and cream had done it. Alcohol is the great leveler. Given a stiff drink, the true descendant of princes boasts of it as if it were not true, the multimillionaire feels poor, and Tristan talks to you about Isolde like a pimp, I said to myself. My malice was beginning to keep pace with my companion's folly.

"I spoiled her myself," he continued. "That's why she's so restless. Damn it, Tower, for years now she's kept me on the go like a gypsy. We've done everything." He held up one large moist freckled hand and counted on its unsteady fingers the things they had done: salmon fishing and photography and pig-sticking and now hawking. They had also been everywhere, and he counted places too, with a boastful as well as pathetic intonation: Norway and America and Java and Morocco and Africa—to say nothing of that winter when she had insisted on Irish rebellion, the most expensive thing on earth.

"I've let her have all my money," he said proudly. "She isn't as pretty as she was; but you know, I let her go to London for all her dresses, or Paris; and she has two maids. Before I married her I had a man to look after me; I gave him up. Now we need this chauffeur, Ricketts, because we're always on the go. I have to keep an eye on him too, because he has an eye for a pretty woman. Funny thing, one day when we were shooting in Scotland with those Americans, I thought Ricketts was insolent about Mrs. Cullen, and I'd have killed him. But she said I imagined it."

All alcoholism in a nutshell, I foolishly mused. And while he, poor man, counted his sports and his travels on his fingers, I meanly ticked off the drunkard's faults and pitfalls of drink as it were on my fingers —indiscretion and boastfulness and snobbism; and sentimentality so nervous that it may switch any minute to the exact opposite; and the sexual note and the sadistic note, undesirable desire, improbable murder. All of it of course a bit unreal and unrealizable in fact ...

What exaggeration I had drifted into! Cullen really was not in very bad shape; I have spent afternoons with a hundred drunker men. The point is that I exaggerated at the time, item by item as he talked along; and I think he sensed it and played up to it: a fatalist and a play-actor. The presence of my fastidious Alex and his overwrought wife downstairs—my wishing they would hurry up and join us, and my dreading it at the same time—made his loose talk more exciting than it would have been in ordinary circumstances. I had been too happy all afternoon, thinking meanwhile of unhappiness; which is a heady combination. Sometimes I am as sensitive as a woman to others' temper or temperament; and it is a kind of sensitivity which may turn, almost by chance, for them or against them. Perhaps at the end of our tête-à-tête I was not much soberer than my companion.

I began to wonder whether, after all, he was not going to tell me the little tale of anxiety or jealousy that winter in London which Alex had half told me in the park. And then he did.

"That winter in London one of our patriots," he began, "had the insolence to fall in love with my wife. A brute of a young fellow named McVoy who was a poet. It got very sticky then. I made up my mind to show them the door, the lot of them. But the more I worried about it, the easier it was for my wife to get around me and have her own way. I didn't want to be unjust to her; and if I'd made a scene before I knew what was up, you see, I might never have known. Terrible, the power a woman has over a man of my nature. You see that side of it, don't you?"

He told it tranquilly enough, though with some breathing between words. He reached out and grasped the cocktail shaker; and having helped himself, kept a tight hold on it. Once or twice he slipped off the tall stool and took steps up and down, carrying the shaker with him instead of his glass, to gesture with; coming back to drink and refill. I had not poured any of this second shakerful for myself; it was almost empty. The whites of his eyes grew more and more untidy, the hazel pupils a harder color; sense of humor and self-knowledge dying down in them. The strong though puffy fingers fixed on the large silver vessel, melting the frostiness off it in patches. I thought of wresting it away from him; emptying it slyly down the little chromium sink; perhaps pretending to be getting drunk myself, and jollying and bullying him along downstairs ... Naturally I did nothing; I looked and listened; I nodded. I wiped the copper top of the bar more than it needed, like a bartender. Probably even bartenders feel a little ignominious curiosity amid their professional boredom.

"One fine day there had to be an end of it, McVoy and all that. Especially one night. The police misunderstood something about him, and were waiting for him at his lodgings; so we had to put him up for the night. I couldn't sleep a wink. I kept hearing him sneaking around in the dark after my wife, I thought. All imagination; I've too much imagination anyway. My wife and I shared a bedroom; we always do; and he'd never have had the courage to come in there.

"Then I had a disgusting dream. I woke up standing beside my wife's bed. There was a moon, and I could see her, and she was sleeping. But I couldn't sleep. So about three o'clock I got up and took a knife from the butler's pantry. I thought I'd tackle McVoy with it. But my wife woke up and came and followed me, across the hall. When she saw the knife naturally it frightened her terribly. And the funny thing was, she frightened me too: there on the landing in her white nightgown. She made me give her the knife and go back to our bedroom. The wonder is we didn't wake McVoy. If we had, there'd have been an awful fuss, I expect. But he slept through it all. Or perhaps he was listening and hiding, scared, under his bed.

"After that I think my wife saw my point of view about it, and was sorry for me. She wept, and it wasn't like her to weep. In a way I was sorry for her too. Think of it, Tower! Think of a common little fellow like that coming to your house, whinnying like a horse around a respectable married woman. He'd have had only himself to blame if I had knifed him. After that Mrs. Cullen sent them all packing, believe me. All the rebels."

He picked up the shaker and shook it hopefully. Now there was only the clunk of small ice in diluted cream, to which I was deaf: a poor host at last, now that it was too late. My feeling about it all really was an absurd mixture. I felt a certain compassion; all the world loves a lover, and especially I do. I also longed to laugh aloud and to tease him. I also itched to tell him the miserable truth about himself, and rather vengefully than for the good it might do. There are a number of circumstances in which the truth does no good; and oh, this was one. I began to feel a mixture of sadness with my malice; a fellow feeling in spite of myself.

Drunkenness does superimpose a certain peculiarity and opaqueness of its own—monotonous complexion, odd aroma, pitch of voice, and nervous twitch— on the rest of a man's humanity; over the personality that you have known sober. But worse still is the transparency and the revelation, as it were sudden little windows uncurtained, or little holes cut, into common recesses of character. It is an anatomy lesson: behold the ducts and sinuses and bladders of the soul, common to every soul ever born! Drunken tricks are nothing but basic human traits. Ordinary frame of mind is never altogether unlike this babble of morbid Irishman. I felt the sickish embarrassment of being mere human clay myself. It seems to me that only art has the right to make one feel that. I am inclined to detest anyone who makes me feel it, as you might say, socially.

"God, Tower, it's tragic," my man sighed. "There's always something. Now I have to keep an eye on our damned Ricketts." He kept it on me for a while then, flashing it or rolling it; sometimes as simply as Othello, sometimes with the imagination and abstraction of a eunuch.

"You know, Tower, it's very interesting. My wife and I are the ideal married couple, so to speak. It's real love. She wouldn't look at another man. I'm as good a man as ever in spite of my age; it runs in the family; and I understand women. Oh, it's not all roses; it never was all roses. There were times when I thought I'd leave her, after some of the mistreatment she's given me. At least I could pretend to, and she might learn to treat me better. All it would need to summon her back would be a wink and a beckoning. She'd do it; she'd stoop her proud neck, I tell you; she'd come on her hands and knees. But I'd never humiliate her, Tower; I never have. To me she's still the proud ignorant girl as I married her; the prettiest in all Dublin.

"The worst mistreatment I've had to bear, you know, is this hawk. There are things only a common fellow could bear peaceably, and a hawk is one of 'em. Funny about hawks, you know, they can't learn to control themselves. They make their messes when they feel the need. Oh, well, you saw it with your own eyes; I sympathized with you. It happens in the hotel, the maids mop up after it, and I can't tell you how ashamed I am. I can't look the man at the desk in the face; he might make a joke of it. Madeleine has to tell him what we want; I won't go near him . . . Funny about women, isn't it? They haven't the same natural shame about things that men have. Let's face it: that's why the church has to keep them in their place, they can't help it. I suppose if they had finer feelings, we men would get left out in the cold, wouldn't we? They'd have none of our kisses. So there you are.

"My wife's a fine trainer of hawks; her crooked old Hungarian admits it himself. But that is one way she can't subdue 'em; it's their nature. She can't teach me much either. She's got to get rid of that hawk, pretty quick; I won't stand for it. You see, I love her, Tower; that's the trouble. Suppose I want to put my arm around her, and she has that hawk on her arm. Can I? No, Larry, no, dear, you'll break a feather, a very important flight feather! Day after day now on the way to Hungary I'll have to sit there pushed over in the corner of the back seat out of Lucy's way; and I tell you, it makes me sick.

"She's been keeping it in our bedroom, because it doesn't like the bathroom. She's sorry for it. I lie awake all night hearing it stir on the perch, and I never forget it for a minute. When I'm beginning to fall asleep I think it's coming to attack me with its nasty beak. You can't imagine what it means to me. I dream of it. I dream sometimes it's an obscene thing; and that wakes me and I reach my arm over to my wife's bed; but she's asleep and takes no notice of me. I tell you, it's not healthy. I dream sometimes it's death. You know, I had an old uncle who saw ghosts, in a big house we had in Galway. I inherited that kind of feeling, you see, and Lucy brings it on. I'll tell you another dream. When I was a boy my old nurse taught me to weave osier baskets; and the other night I dreamed Lucy was a basket. Her feathers weren't right for it because they were sticky, but I wove her; and I gave her to my wife. But this is the end! No more Lucy!"

That was a lovely moment, to my way of thinking. My animosity toward this fool husband suddenly wafted away. It is a manner of self-revelation that I especially delight in: by means of loose imagery, and dreams, and careless connection of odd bits of memory as they come. Even as he spoke I hoped that I should be able to remember every word.

For alcohol is a god, as the Greeks decided when it was first introduced from the East, although a god of vengeance. The drinker becomes the drunkard. Everyone is to blame. The soberest man or woman in the world at some time or another has helped the sad process along in some poor dear drinker's case. For example, I think someone must have looked at Cullen in his youth when drunkenness became him, and so loved or admired him in it that he began to regard that as the secret of love and admiration. There are men who master the trick of drink, and practically never take a drop without being made admirable by it. I have known one or two; they were extraordinary men in other ways as well.

But even for the average man, even in the poorest booze-fight—between the vanity of the beginning and the sickness at last—there is a fine moment. It is the mark of its oriental origin and the proof of the Greek belief in it. The fumes seem suddenly mixed with more light and air than usual, and it is the right mixture. The silly self-consciousness clears up; the chip falls from the shoulder. Your friend is drinking, and you are not, or not much; so naturally there is an undercurrent of quarrel between you; now suddenly it ceases, peaceful. His tipsy mind is as it were sitting quiet, like an oracle on a tripod, under the influence not of alcohol simply, but of himself, his very nature, his fatality, his childhood. Whatever has been kept secret, damped in ashes, smothered and contemptible, begins to come out; and for the average man there is no harm in it. The murderous man may murder then, the madman talk nonsense; who cares? For most of us the ashes are bad, the secrecy mistaken, the contempt and self-contempt contemptible—and the raking of the ashes is good. For a moment, drunk as a lord, instead of coarseness and looseness you have the intuition of a child or an old woman . . .

Of course it does not last long. Ordinarily when it has occurred, befuddlement and some bodily incompetence are in the offing. Too much delight in it may cause one to keep the worst company in the world all one's life. But certainly it is one of the main things in human nature, worth experiencing and worth watching. Cullen did not quite reach it that afternoon, on vodka and cream in Alex's silly de luxe bar. But I thought he was about to, when we were interrupted. As I really did not like him anyway I did not care much.

It was Alex who interrupted us, coming into the big room under the balcony and calling to me. She wanted me to visit Jean and Eva in the kitchen, and encourage them about the impromptu dinner and hurry them up. She had been hearing strange tones of voice out there; and she was afraid that if she went herself, Jean might make speeches and Eva might weep.

It was a large, unmistakably French kitchen: the stove in a deep niche of brick; dim walls and array of copper; the open doorway and windows full of little landscape with afternoon sunlight slanting across it. The Cullens' chauffeur was there with our two servants, and somehow it seemed to me dramatic as well as picturesque. Jean was the classic manservant, a type that you find more or less the same all around the Mediterranean: doubtless very good-looking and amorous as a boy; forty now and the worse for wear, with a bald spot and dark jowls and several teeth missing; a man broken to harness but still apt to show off his emotions, and still amorous. He had acquired Eva in Morocco; and she certainly had Moorish blood though she called herself Italian. She was half his age and lovely, although of an increasing billowy fatness; pale in the way that seems sallow at times, silvery at other times. Ricketts was a fine Cockney, bright-eyed and sharp-nosed. He sat at the table in the middle of the room in a spoiled young male attitude, with a bottle of wine half empty and half a plate of Eva's little Moorish cakes.

Dinner was flourishing; that I could tell by the smell of it. Along with which I breathed the early summer wafting in: a tart exhalation of the sod, a scent of some shrub that was like a dark candy. In spite of the open door, the stove going full tilt for the squabs and the strawberry tart made the room hot, which brought out the men's untidy healthy body odor. Eva had one of those cheap North African perfumes in a little cake like a rubber eraser, and had put that on to excess, which, alas, I fancied, was for the young Englishman's benefit. And the mood of the room, the morality or psychology of the three together, was as confusing as this fragrant air in it. Eva stood and stared at Ricketts. Her great eyes were a little reddened; probably she had been weeping; at the moment she was smiling vaguely. Ricketts poured the sour red wine down his throat half a glass at a time; and between throatfuls looked up at her with a becoming brightness. Jean pretended to be busy beside the stove with his back to them. But he agitated the pots and pans, and flashed glances over his shoulder, and replied to my questions about the tart and the cheese with a little more obscurity and more assurance than I liked.

Then I happened to look outdoors. It pleased me to be able to see, in a little interval between two shrubs, the dreamy hawk hunched up on the rustic bench. And then, to my amazement, I saw Cullen on the left coming across the lawn. Very slowly, with a kind of noticeable alcoholic endeavor not to be noticed; on tiptoe, and as if the grass were a loud and slippery surface like a ballroom floor . . . Instantly I sensed that it was abnormal and scandalous. But I could not run out to see what he was up to, without making a little scandal myself. Jean and Eva and Ricketts would follow or at least watch. So there I stood, acting absent-minded, murmuring about the Camembert and the iced hock.

Cullen vanished for a moment behind one of those two shrubs near Lucy's perch. When he reappeared he was crouching, and hitching along on the balls of his feet, and steadying himself with one hand, closer and closer to her. The grotesque furtive approach indicated for one thing that he had no rational plan, no serious intention. For Lucy was hooded as well as leashed; she could not see him. He kept stretching out one hand, very tense; but he could scarcely have reached her from that quadruped position. I began to think it funny. But from the bedroom window Alex and Mrs. Cullen could have seen him as well as I: that was a pity . . .

Perhaps it occurred to him. He scrambled to his feet, and somewhat assumed an attitude of knowing what he was about, and leaned over the bench with his back to me. Perhaps he was undoing the knot or knots of the leash. Evidently he was not alarming Lucy much; she opened her wings a few inches, as if expecting to be picked up. But he drew back, and to my dismay, my disgust, thrust his hand in his pocket and brought out a large pocketknife and opened it. Murder at last, I thought. It was Lucy's turn; no more Lucy!

Before I even got started to run out and stop him, he simply pushed her hard off the back of the bench, re-coiling away from her at the same time. It was obvious how afraid of her he was. With a large indignant flut-ter she landed on the grass. He had cut the leash; he had not cut her throat. Also he had unhooded her. On the grass for a moment she took a rapid confused look in every direction. Then with a great lift of her legs and two or three strokes of her wings, she climbed up on top of the air, and above the lawn, and across the pond. It was lovely. Her searching looks still, this way and that—to discover why she had been loosed, what quarry there was for her—made her appear to be shaking her head, saying no, no.

I lost sight of her when she passed behind a tree; again, when she rose beyond the scope of the kitchen window. Down she came then, with neck and wing and tail and legs all out—in the shape of a six-pointed star, big and dim, collapsing. She rested her weight on the air again for an instant, and alighted on a post in the far corner of the garden. It was one of two posts from which Eva hung Alex's lingerie to dry early in the morning. The gesture of alighting was lovely: her rigid hands clutching the top of the post like a living victim. It might have been a little angel seizing a tall man by the hair. Then there she sat, still wondering what in the world—what, in terms of a hawk's simple murderous instinct—this liberation meant.

Meanwhile, of course Cullen too had gazed up at her, gazed across the pond at her. Now like a ninny he waved good-bye, good-bye. Then he turned and ambled back through the bushes. Jean and Eva and Ricketts, in their matrimonial or adulterous absorption, had not seen a thing. I was thankful for that; I also felt a childish optimism because of it. I waited a bit, to give Cullen time to get settled in the living room. Then I dashed out of the kitchen, and knocked at Alex's bedroom door, and shouted through it to Mrs. Cullen. I simply said that Lucy was no longer on her perch. Then I hastened away to see what state of mind Cullen was in. There he sat in the living room, one leg over the arm of his easy chair, stoutly puffing; sorrowful and also smug, I thought, and somewhat sobered by his exploit; that at least was a blessing.

"The hawk has got loose. It's not on the bench. I've called Mrs. Cullen. She's coming to look for it. It must have untied the leash itself." I said this as emphatically as I could, to suggest to him the line he should take.

"But what about the hood?" he asked in an infuriating little tone. "I cut the leash myself, damn it all."

Whereupon I groaned or I cursed; I can't remember

which. I didn't want him to confess; I should have spoken to him before I called his wife; now it was too late. She came rushing from the bedroom; and it was as if the news had instantly disheveled her from head to foot. She shuffled, her fine shoes half unlaced. Her perfect dress hung or clung around her one-sidedly. She was pulling on the blood-stained gauntlet; and as she crossed the room she impatiently ran her other hand up through her hair, which fell down on that side over her cheek. She did not close her mouth between her voluble exclamations. "Damn, damn. Oh, I am so unhappy. I must get her back, I can't bear to lose her."

At the sight of her, Cullen pulled himself up out of the easy chair and stood at a kind of attention: but badly, not a bit brave. She must have seen him; she took no notice. I had a sense of her knowing what had happened, who had done it. She looked like the type of old Irishwoman who has second sight: countrified, frumpy, and frightened. And in spite of her outcries and panicky movements, it seemed to me that she had an air of experience and familiarity; familiarity with fright.

"Oh, Mr. Tower, can you get me the other half of that pigeon?" she begged. "The pigeon I fed her. She hasn't, I hope she hasn't, gone far away."

Upon which her husband behind us chimed in

as usual, worse than usual: "Madeleine, Madeleine, surely they've cooked it. That's the dinner, you know, pigeons with white currants."

She took notice of that. She swung around and answered in a devilish voice, "Of course they have not cooked it." For one second I thought she might strike him; perhaps he did too. He wrinkled his nose and flung up his hands.

I started toward the kitchen and she followed, explaining, "I'll never catch her without a lure. Thank heaven it was a small pigeon, she'll still be hungry." She gave me a perhaps affectionate pat on the shoulder which amounted to a push.

Then she ran back to the window, and there gave a wonderful small shriek. It should have been hawklike, I said to myself; what it really made me think of was a valkyrie, a very small valkyrie. For in spite of my admiration of Lucy and sympathy for the other two, I was enjoying all this.

I met Alex at the kitchen door, and she had the half-pigeon. Mrs. Cullen called to us, "What in God's name did I do with my bag? My extra leash is in it. She must have broken hers."

Alex ran for the bag, handing me the pigeon. I dropped it, and it smudged the parquet. Jean and Eva were there beside me, but they were too thrilled to do any mopping now. Then Mrs. Cullen lost one shoe and stumbled into an armchair; and her husband knelt and tried to put it back on, fumbling around her silky ankle with those freckled fingers which could so easily have snapped it in two like a twig—until she lost patience and kicked the other shoe off, over his shoulder, and rose to go in her stocking-feet.

"Stay here, all of you," she ordered. "Please, please, let me go alone." She paused a moment on the threshold staring across the pond at heedless Lucy. She held her gloved fingers up to her mouth as you do when you blow a kiss. Then she swung around toward us, demanding, with a kind of loud lump in her throat, "Where in God's name is her hood? How wicked! Who did it? One of you, how wicked!"

It was poor Eva who answered, with her primitive sensibility, primitive expectation of blame: "Oh, Madame, Madame, Jean and I never left the kitchen," and began to cry.

Alex told her to hush, which she did, more or less. As I watched our angry birdcatcher, I still kept one eye on these other watchers, so assorted and attractive, there inside the house in a row close to the plate-glass window in the last murky sunshine. I thought that Alex glanced oddly back at me; perhaps my eyewitnessing and slight complicity had given me an odd expression. Certainly she hated this disorder: obscure common blundering around her house, and general self-betrayal, with the servants goggle-eyed. On the other hand catching a great runaway bird was the sort of problem she loved. Her mild brown eyes lit up, and she breathed like a happy child. Ricketts came tip-toeing in and stood behind us as close to Eva as he dared. Whereupon Jean began whispering to her in Italian, *prestissimo*, until Alex hushed him too. Eva dabbed her eyes with the corner of the towel, another corner of which had pigeon's blood on it. As for Cullen, his face was quite mottled with his mixed emotions; heaven knows what they were.

As Mrs. Cullen left us, across the lawn, along the left side of the pond, I was struck by the change this emergency had made in her appearance and carriage. Perhaps it was chiefly her going in stocking-feet. When she first descended from the Daimler, how delicately she had stumbled on the cobblestones; then foolishly tripped back and forth on the waxed parquet, and weakly strolled in the park! That French or Italian footwear of hers with three-inch heels not only inca-pacitated her but flattered her, and disguised her. Now her breasts seemed lower on her torso, out of the way of her nervous arms. Her hips were wide and her back powerful, with that curve from the shoulder blades to the head which you see in the nudes of Ingres. She walked with her legs well apart, one padding footfall after another, as impossible to trip up as a cat.

Suddenly she must have remembered that she had brought an extra leash but no extra hood. She hurried back along the water and across to the rustic bench, where she picked up the one Cullen had removed and let fall; then set out again, by the right bank, more slow and catlike as she approached her quarry. What followed took only a few moments. We heard the falconer's cry: *hai, hai,* a desolate sound, which probably has not varied much in the three or four thousand years of falconry, for it is based on eternal acoustics, agreeable to the changeless ears of hawks. I loved to hear it. Lucy's head stirred swiftly around in response to it. I wanted her to cry back, *aik,* which she did not. They were too far away for us to see much. We saw the swing of Mrs. Cullen's arm as she tossed the piece of the pigeon over the hedge, toward the foot of the post; and after a breathless instant, we saw Lucy's descent upon it, down in one smooth rush, like a large, dusky, finished flower off its stem. Instantly the birdcatcher bent over, lurked along the hedge, and squattingly slipped around behind it. Then we had to wait, wait— until she briskly stood up and started back toward us with Lucy hooded on her wrist, where she belonged.

Before hooding her, I suppose, she let her have a few good beakfuls of the unscheduled pigeon so that even this mishap or misdemeanor should be a lesson to her, as it was to us all in a sense.

Inside the house, before the great window, we were smiling from ear to ear, and murmuring or exclaiming each in his or her way. Only Cullen was deathly still, not even puffing. I moved far enough away from him to see his face, and found there, added to the bibulous pink, a pale light of wild relief, reprieve, even rapture, as if that horrid bird on his wife's arm returning to haunt him again had been his heart's desire. It was too much of a good thing; he was sober perhaps, but tormentedly sentimental; I should not have trusted him an instant.

Mrs. Cullen came down the left side of the pond, the long way. The sun, muffled all afternoon, was setting brightly. Some of its beams turned back up from the water, broken into a sparkle, through which we could not see her well. There were vague irises and something else up to her ankles; and branches of lilac occasionally hung between us and her. Her face looked to me calm, careless. Her hair still absurdly fell down one cheek; now and then she blew it out of her eyes. Dress disarranged and petticoat showing and stocking-feet and all, she walked back proudly, taking her time; a springy walk that reminded me of Isadora Duncan.

The five of us happy onlookers trooped out on the lawn to meet her. "Isn't it wonderful?" she rejoiced. "You see, she's perfectly manned. She understands. Otherwise I could never have caught her. I'll be hunting with her in no time. Larry, go and find the other leash; which I left on the bench." And she decidedly emphasized the I. She too wished him not to admit what he had done.

He went meekly for the leash. The servants returned to the kitchen. Mrs. Cullen asked permission to retire and put herself to rights, declining Alex's offer of company and assistance. "No more weathering for you, my haggard Lucy," I heard her mutter as she left us.

I had not dared hope that Lucy—haggard that she was, with only two months of the least comfortable phase of captivity to look back upon, and none of the pleasure of the chase so far, and one toe still sore from the trap—would allow herself to be caught. That had made the little spectacle of her capture or surrender the more exciting for me. On the other hand I had not wanted her to escape. I had not pictured her setting out lonelily over Normandy toward Scotland, or whatever resort in the summer she might instinctively choose. Given my sentimental imagination, it was an odd lapse. And it made me aware of my really not wanting Larry Cullen to escape from Mrs. Cullen either, or vice versa. Perhaps I do not believe in liberty, or I regard it as only episodic in life; a circumstance that one must be able to bear and profit by when it occurs; a kind of necessary evil. When love itself is at stake, love of liberty as a rule is only fear of captivity.

Alex thought a drink would help at this juncture, and started to the balcony; but with one glance in Cullen's direction and another in mine, she returned and sat down. Cullen slumped in his armchair, gazing at apparently nothing, in that calm which is only the entire expenditure of energy; the coming down of a dull curtain upon the drama in head or heart. But probably it was only entr'acte. There was something turgid if not turbulent throughout his aging bulky frame; his jaws stirred a bit in his double chin; his bloodshot eyes kept lighting up.

Then we heard a persistent ringing of the bell in Alex's room, and Alex went anxiously to see what it meant, and came back and informed us that Mrs. Cullen had decided to return to town at once, before dinner. She had a brother in Paris, and she had telephoned him; something had gone wrong in Paris, and he needed her. I did not believe a word of this, and Alex's expression confirmed my disbelief. Evidently it did not surprise Cullen. He sighed hard, which perhaps referred to *pigeons aux groseilles*; but he said nothing even about that.

Alex left it to me to inform Jean and Eva of the superfluity of their dinner. I could scarcely tell how Eva took it, not well in any case: she gaped at me and fled to her bedroom. Jean on the other hand chose to be superior and calm. Something always went wrong, he observed, when the English upper classes came to see poor Mademoiselle, in their automobiles as big as buses driven by idiotic little boys. In his opinion also the boy Ricketts had something to do with the escape of Madame Cullen's eagle. At that moment the idiot was paying a visit to the *bistrot* or bar at the corner. I let Jean go after him. The announcement of the Cullens' change of plan might somewhat relieve his evident personal desire to put him out of the house.

Meanwhile with a certain simplicity our unhappy guests gathered up their belongings here and there: severed leash and mislaid lipstick and cigarette case with a diamond button. As we waited in the hallway for the Daimler to be brought around Mrs. Cullen quietly asked, "Dear Alex, you don't need a new chauffeur, do you?"

As it happened Alex did need one. "What luck! I wish you'd take Ricketts," Mrs. Cullen quietly continued.

"I'll be giving him notice when we get to Budapest. And I know he hates Ireland, and he speaks quite decent French. He's very good, very fast, and a mechanic and all that." And she recommended him in other particulars as well, including semi-genteel birth.

Cullen beside me was shuffling and loudly hemming, and at last could not hold his peace. "But Madeleine, really, my dear woman, you're fantastic. We've never had anybody as good as Ricketts. What in the world!"

Slightly embarrassed, Alex said that indeed they might have difficulty in finding a chauffeur in Hungary in summer; it should not be decided in haste on her account. Perhaps she sensed what was coming; I did.

"Oh, I shall easily find another," Mrs. Cullen said, "or I can do without. You see, Ricketts doesn't like Lucy. He laughs at me up his sleeve. I doubtless am an old fool, but I cannot have people around me who think so." She said this in a great sad false way; and it was unmistakably intended for her husband.

Again I could not see his banal but significant face when I wished, to read the emotion in it; we stood shoulder to shoulder facing our dear women. There was still some of that fine pre-bolshevik distillation on his somewhat accelerated and audible breath; but its troublesome effects must have passed. We all kept silent for a moment.

Mrs. Cullen was quite willing to look either of us in the eye; but her sparkle was all extinguished. It would have seemed healthier, more rational, if her eyes had looked angry; they looked nothing at all, nullified. Lucy was hooded now; under her mistress's chin the frivolous topknot on the stitched leather nodded very slightly; and Mrs. Cullen's crooked Irish face as a whole was not much more expressive than that. Her serenity, her stoical wit, her obscurity, were a sort of mental or moral craftsmanship; ornamentation. Inside all that, I suspected, her spirit was as blind as Lucy's. The point of not allowing a hawk to see is to keep it from being frightened; and I hoped that Mrs. Cullen's grand, mean manner served that purpose as well. I was afraid it did not.

Along the cobblestones under the plane trees I heard the Daimler come purring, not a moment too soon. By that time I also felt—as it seemed, aching in my bones and running in my veins and tempering my nerves—something like the mixture of hot and cold, good and bad, which troubled the difficult hearts of this odd couple.

Unrequited passion; romance put asunder by circumstances or mistakes; sexuality pretending to be love—all that is a matter of little consequence, a mere voluntary temporary uneasiness, compared with the long course of true love, especially marriage. In marriage, insult arises again and again and again; and pain has to be not only endured, but consented to; and the amount of forgiveness that it necessitates is incredible and exhausting. When love has given satisfaction, then you discover how large a part of the rest of life is only payment for it, installment after installment . . . That was the one definite lesson which these petty scenes of the Cullens illustrated. Early in life I had learned it for myself well enough. It was on Alex's account that I minded. To see the cost of love before one has felt what it is worth is a pity; one may never have the courage to begin.

There stood the Daimler; and Cullen and I helped Mrs. Cullen and Lucy up into it, while Ricketts, cap in hand, held the door. I observed that in fact Ricketts was laughing, in a silent subaltern way; but surely it was not at his mistress or her bird. Thin lips very red, rough eyelashes very shadowy: the effect of a Moorish-Italian kiss behind the kitchen door, I fancied. Or perhaps—for Cockneys are a malicious breed—the mere discomfiture of Jean amused him. He glanced over my shoulder, then up at a likely window, and so did I; but I did not discover the Mediterranean couple peeping out anywhere.

Neither the Cullens nor Alex and I had the heart

for much repetition of farewell. Cullen had tears in his eyes. We turned back to the house and shut the door before Ricketts could get the long car out onto the highway, amid cars coming toward him from Paris.

There had been just time for us to reach the living room and sit down and light cigarettes, when we heard a fearful grinding of brakes; then several cars honking as in panic; and a Frenchman shouting the usual insults. A moment after, a car drove in under our plane trees. I got up and looked out a small window on that side: it was the Daimler.

Alex and I hastened back through the hall to see what had happened. There we heard Mrs. Cullen's voice, very loud and exclamatory but incomprehensible; and she was pushing the doorbell, rattling the doorknob, and calling, "Alex, Alex!" As I opened the door she stepped back, turning away from us, gesticulating and exclaiming, "No, Ricketts, stay where you are. Larry, please! Now wait for me, Ricketts. Oh, dear, you fool, you fool!"

She stumbled on the cobblestones; Lucy was having a hard time. Then she returned to us and grasped Alex's arm and motioned us back inside the house. "Don't get out of the car, Larry, I'll attend to it," she cried, over her shoulder.

"Alex, dear, I'm sorry, I've forgotten something.

Poor damned fool," she repeated. By the heartbroken
tone of her voice I judged that the fool was not Ricketts.

That young man was not laughing now, nor smack-
ing his lips upon any recollection of pleasure or rivalry.
His lips were white; he was badly frightened. The
Daimler stood at a very odd angle between two trees;
he must have made a U-turn on the highway. A little
farther along on the verge of a ditch stood an old
Renault, with which, I supposed, they had narrowly
escaped a collision. Its French driver stood beside
it, still vehemently expressing himself, shaking his
fist. But, oddly, neither the Cullens nor Ricketts even
glanced in that Frenchman's direction. Something else
must have happened; just before, just after, or at the
same time. Inside the Daimler, Cullen had his great
hand pressed over his mouth as if he were gnawing it,
and he too was pale: the worst pallor in the world, like
cooked veal. During the little drama of recapturing
Lucy he had ceased to be drunk, I thought. But now I
was afraid that he was going to be sick.

Alex and I followed Mrs. Cullen inside the house.
She too was in a worse emotion and looked worse
than before. Not only a portion of her lovely hair but
her hat as well this time hung over one ear. There
were beads of sweat on her brow and her upper lip.
"Oh, Alex, do forgive us," she kept saying, "I'm so

ashamed, so ashamed"; and hurried past us into the living room.

Shame, I must say, was one thing which all this did not suggest. Across that great expanse of waxed parquet toward the garden door she sped ahead of us—her pretty feet on her too high heels wide apart, lest she skid and fall headlong—saying to Alex over her shoulder, "Excuse me. Please, dear. Don't mind me. Let me go into the garden alone a minute."

On her wrist of course Lucy still perched, that is, rode, with some difficulty: her green-gold feet also wide apart, ducking or dipping to keep her balance, with characteristic indignation of her shoulders and that nervous puffing of breast-feathers which, as Mrs. Cullen had informed us, is a good sign in a hunting hawk. Hawks are not really tree-birds; and if in a state of nature Lucy had ever found herself on a perch as agitated as this female arm, blown by any such passionate wind as this, whatever this was—she would have left it instantly and sought out a rock. It was absurd. Even her little blind headgear with parrot feathers seemed to me absurd; it matched the French hat which her mistress was wearing at so Irish an angle, except that it was provided with secure drawstrings. In spite of my bewilderment and alarm, I began to laugh. It struck me as a completion of the cycle of the afternoon, an end of the sequence of meanings I had been reading into everything, especially Lucy. The all-embracing symbolic bird; primitive image with iron wings and rusty tassels and enameled feet; airy murderess like an angel; young predatory sanguinary de luxe hen—now she was funny; she had not seemed funny before. Perhaps all pets, all domesticated animals, no matter how ancient or beautiful or strange, show a comic aspect sooner or later; a part of the shame of our humanity that we gradually convey to them.

Just then I saw what Mrs. Cullen had in her right hand, half concealed against her breast and behind Lucy's wing: a large revolver. Alex must have seen it before I did. She was clinging to my elbow and whispering, "Stay back. Don't laugh, don't follow her."

I am not a judge of firearms, but this was a grim important object, glimmering, apparently brand-new and in working order. "Shall I try to take it away from her?" I asked Alex in a whisper.

"Heavens, no. She'll be all right. Don't worry her." Women, even some young girls, have this ability to guess at degrees of trouble; this equanimity of a trained nurse. And, with or without much affection, they sometimes suddenly know each other as if they were twins.

There was more to it than that. Looking back on that moment I have wondered just how her friend's passion appeared to Alex. How could she tell, as the disheveled creature fled ahead of us into the garden, that she was not going to kill herself? Then it occurred to me that in my friend's character and way of life in those days there was a certain passivity; at least abstention from others' lives. Whatever she did not understand about them might, she felt, be more awful than anything she could imagine. If others said that things were unbearable, she could well believe it. If the Irishwoman's life had reached that point, the point of suicide, I think she might not have cared to interfere or prevent it.

Outside on the terrace Mrs. Cullen stopped; and grasping the gun by the barrel, brought it back over her shoulder and hurled it high above the shrubs, far across the lawn, so that it splashed into the pond.

This important gesture was too much for Lucy. Off the dear wrist she went, hung in a paroxysm once more. But this time it was not bating, not mystical dread or symbolical love of liberty; it was just ordinary loss of balance. Symbol or no symbol, I said to myself, if I were busy getting rid of a suicidal or murderous weapon I should hate to have a heavy hysterical bird tied to me, yanking my wrist, flapping in my face. Mrs. Cullen, the good sportswoman, did not mind. Perhaps because of her own hysteria—the real meaning of this episode pulling at her heartstrings and beating upon her intellect—she merely did the thing to do, as usual. Up went her embattled left arm over her head; stock-still she stood, until terrible Lucy grew tired, and recovered her self-control, and resumed her domestication.

From our viewpoint, behind her, seeing her through the sunset-streaked window, against the background of the old park and the shrubs and the gray pond with ripples unclosing away from the place where the gun had gone down, Mrs. Cullen was beautiful. Throughout her somewhat bulky body—motherly torso and panting breast and round neck—there was wonderful strength; and between her absurd high heels and her fist in the rough glove, there was exact perpendicularity: the yard-wind wings now settling back on top. And the fact that she looked a bit ridiculous, disheveled and second-rate and past her prime, made it all the finer, I thought, as she turned and came slowly back indoors.

There were tears in her eyes, but she chuckled, or pretended to, or tried to. "Darling Alex," she said hoarsely, "did you ever have guests who behaved so madly? Don't, please, don't ever ask me what this was all about."

Then in her way, in a series of little dull, prosaic,

but shameless statements, she told us what it was about. "You see, dear, why we can't live in Ireland. It's such a bad example for my silly sons."

My presence did not make her shy. For a moment that flattered me; upon second thought it seemed to me to have the opposite implication. Quite early in the afternoon, I suppose, she had perceived that Alex was not in love with me; therefore, in her view of life, I did not count, I was a supernumerary. What harm could I do with her secrets? Women are fantastic.

Holding her left arm and Lucy well out of the way, she threw her right arm somewhat around Alex and kissed her. "Dear, dear friend," she murmured. "You're so clever, you'll marry well when the time comes. Thank you so much for your patience with us." Alex shrank a little as she always did from female affection, but the odd compliment seemed to please her.

"Larry's been threatening to leave me for weeks," Mrs. Cullen added. "Oh, I'm so afraid he will one day. I don't know what would become of him by himself, the fool, the old darling."

Poor Larry, I sighed; poor supernumerary me! Women are no respecters of men. I also felt a little indignation on Lucy's account. Trapped out of the real wind and rock, and perverted rather than domesticated, kept blind and childish, at the mercy of every human absurdity, vodka and automobiles, guns and kisses: poor Lucy! She no doubt personified for Mrs. Cullen the deep problems of life; certainly Mrs. Cullen now devoted a large part of her life to her. Yet again and again, splendid *falco*'s position in fact, her proprietress's handling of her, was in the way of a handkerchief or a muff or a hat. Absorbed in her narration of what had just occurred on the highway in the Daimler, Mrs. Cullen forgot about her and gestured a little with her left hand as well as her right. Lucy had to embrace the air desperately to stabilize herself; her plumage all thickened up and homely, sick-looking. It afforded me an instant's characteristic grim amusement to think how often the great issues which I had taken this bird to augur come down in fact to undignified appearance, petty neurasthenic anecdote; bring one in fact at last to a poor domestication like Lucy's. It also reminded me of the absurd position of the artist in the midst of the disorders of those who honor and support him, but who can scarcely be expected to keep quiet around him for art's sake.

"I don't even know which of us Larry thought of shooting," Mrs. Cullen said. "Wife or chauffeur or haggard. I dare say I never shall know, unless some day he does it. The minute you closed your door, he began saying things at the top of his voice about Lucy and

Ricketts. It upset Ricketts, and there was a car coming toward us, and for a moment I really thought we would crash. I told Ricketts to stop at the side of the road, and instead he turned back here, with two other cars speeding around the corner. That was what made the little Frenchman in the Renault angry. In the midst of which poor Larry began to threaten us with the revolver. It was in the side pocket of the car. I can't imagine when he put it there, or where he got it. You know, I think the Frenchman saw it. Lucky for us he didn't call the police."

She began to have an almost cheerful expression. If you have been lonelily excited a long while, expecting the worst to happen, with no validation for your fear in fact, no excuse that others would understand— perhaps the trouble in question must always come as a slight relief. At least you know then that you have not morbidly made it all up out of whole cloth.

"I'll tell you an odd thing about myself," she said, with her vaguest smile. "I happen to be a very good shot; and d'you know, all the while I was trying to take that beastly gun away from Larry—with Ricketts driving like a fool, and poor Lucy on my arm so awfully in the way—I kept calculating every instant just where the bullet would go if he pulled the trigger. The trajectory and all that. I suppose I'm a born sportswoman;

how childish it is! At the last moment I simply can't take things quite seriously. I suppose that's what made me good at lions in Kenya years ago."

She frowned and sighed then, as if ashamed of her coldness or lightheartedness. "Now Ricketts of course is quite out of patience with Larry. I suppose I shall have to give him notice; what a pity! If Larry wasn't quiet after I got out of the car, I expect Ricketts knocked him out. He did once before. There's nothing I can do; Larry is as strong as an ox. But I'd have gone mad, I'd have killed Ricketts—if I had waited to see what happened. Ricketts is so damned English; the instant he clenches his fist he makes a smug face, like a governess. But I dare say it's time to go back now; I've been cowardly long enough; perhaps at this point I can be of some comfort to my man."

She intended to give Alex another kiss, but Alex avoided it. "Oh, Alex, I do," she lamented, "do love that great fool desperately. Whatever shall I do with him? Oh, well, we'll see. Do you think I must get rid of Lucy? It was astonishing, you know, how well Larry hawked, last summer in Hungary. I thought he'd enjoy it so."

Then she laughed, and all afternoon I think she had not laughed; rather a bad sound, two loud liquid feverish notes. "Ho, ho, perhaps this may have done him good. He has bated, don't you know."

So she took her second departure. "Good-bye, Mr. Tower. Good-bye, Alex, dear child. I shall miss you. Larry will be ashamed to see you after all this, I'm afraid. Don't come out to the car; it would embarrass them." She slipped across the hall and out the door, opening it only a little and immediately slamming it.

"Well!" exclaimed Alex, as we returned to the living room, and her delivery of that syllable made me laugh: ooo-ell; the soft bark of a very small dog.

After so much disorder we thought it would be indiscreet to seem impatient for our dinner. We wandered into the garden, sighing, tired. "I hope Jean and Eva did not see this last bit of melodrama," Alex said. "It's not the kind of idea I should like him to get into his head and develop. He's no Cullen; he's an imitative Italian, and he might not muff it."

"That great comfortable greedy easy old boy," I mumbled, meaning Cullen. "Did you dream he had murder in him? Vodka or no vodka."

"But it was suicide surely, not murder," said Alex. "Madeleine Cullen has no imagination."

"I wonder. It overlaps in any case. People do kill themselves just because they want to murder someone," I replied in my quibbling way. "Someone they love."

Alex made a little face, expressive of skepticism

of everything and practically universal disapproval. "You know, he wasn't really very drunk."

"Two shakerfuls of prewar vodka," I reminded her.

"No matter. That's not much for those immense Irishmen. I've seen him drunk and it wasn't anything like this. Or perhaps he pretended to be drunk for your benefit; and to have an excuse for what was happening anyway, what was bound to happen. You're such a sober creature, my dear; you naturally overestimate other people's intoxication."

Her saying that made me suddenly unhappy. I thought of the wicked way I had watched him as he drank, the grandiose theories of drunkenness I had spun for myself meanwhile; and I blushed. Half the time, I am afraid, my opinion of people is just guessing; cartooning. Again and again I give way to a kind of inexact and vengeful lyricism; I cannot tell what right I have to be avenged, and I am ashamed of it. Sometimes I entirely doubt my judgment in moral matters; and so long as I propose to be a story-teller, that is the whisper of the devil for me.

But my dear Alex then sensed, as a good young woman should, my doubt and weak self-criticism; and she smiled. "You must tell me what he said to you, before you forget it. I gathered from your expression that he'd been weeping on your shoulder."

Then Eva, with even less etiquette than usual, came out of the kitchen waving a napkin, huskily imploring us to hurry in to dinner, half-spoiled in any case, she thought. As if to point the moral of the changes of the day from a cook's angle, Jean sent in to us eight pigeons, a veritable sheaf of asparagus, and two good-sized tarts. It was perfect; and melodrama all afternoon evidently gave us appetite. Eva shed a sequence of tears as she served, mutely and prettily, with a wan smile whenever I looked at her, like a seventeenth-century Magdalen. Jean brought the tart himself and thanked us for our overeating, as if it had been a special effort to console him.

After he had served our coffee in the living room, I told Alex what I had seen from the kitchen window. I was surprised to learn that she too had seen it, from her bedroom window, while Mrs. Cullen lay stretched on the bed with her eyes shut. But she had missed the jackknife. Then I tried to remember and report to her Cullen's confession to me, man to man over our vodka, which entertained her, although I think it shocked her.

Then she went to write a note and send a telegram, and she did not return for three-quarters of an hour. I sat there by myself, not even trying to read. I was still excited; and I fell into a form of fatigued stupidity which, while it lasts, often seems to me an important intellectual effort. It was an effort to compress the excessive details of the afternoon into an abstraction or two, a formula or a moral; in order to store that away in my head for future use, and yet leave room for something new, for the next thing. Morally speaking, those Cullens had crowded me out of myself. I also hoped to distinguish a little more clearly between what the Cullens meant to me and certain fine points of my own meaning to myself which had fascinated me in the midst of their afternoon's performance. Of course it was not possible.

I have learned—but again and again I forget—that abstraction is a bad thing, innumerable and infinitesimal and tiresome; worse than any amount of petty fact. The emotion that comes blurring my retrospect is warmer and weaker than the excitement of whatever happened, good or bad. It is like a useless, fruitless vegetation, spreading and twining and fading and corrupting; even the ego disappears under it . . . Therefore I scarcely noticed how long my dear friend stayed away in her bedroom; and therefore I was glad when she came back. For me, putting a stop to so-called thought is one of the functions of friendship.

It was not writing or telegraphing which had kept her; it was Eva weeping and denouncing Jean, laughing and worshiping Jean. They had quarreled about Ricketts, and after that he had gone to the village to get drunk. He would kill her, he had said, and sooner or later he might well, Eva thought; certainly he would beat her the minute he returned. He was the most jealous man alive, in her opinion, and she worshiped him.

In any case she was much to blame. She had a way of obviously reveling in the sense of her own beauty whenever a new man appeared in the kitchen; a look of being at the mercy of circumstances, or perhaps at the man's mercy. Neighbor or workman or tradesman would appear; and casually Eva would come up, and stand close by, with a sleepy stare, letting her eyes drop sideways in their wide sockets amid African eyelashes, giving off her sweetness like a flower bed— while Jean watched her, admiring and suffering, until his storm broke.

Alex had asked what made her behave so; why she flirted with men like Ricketts if she loved Jean and wanted to be at peace with him. Seriously she had explained that, when she flirted, it gave him a chance to come between her and the rival, which made her feel his love, and to that of course she promptly yielded; and her yielding also gave him assurance that she loved him. "And if you please, terrible female that she is," said Alex, "she laughed as she explained it, deep in her fat throat.

"But she would not go on laughing. This time, she thinks, it has gone too far. He will beat her, and he may kill her, and *tutti quanti*. Therefore she began to cry again, and she wanted to tell me their story again, from the beginning. I pretended to lose my temper and sent her to bed.

"I shall have to dismiss them, you know, if they go on like this," Alex added. "The lower classes have a way of making one ashamed of one's sex."

She always had trouble with servants. The trouble really was that her kind interest in them, if aroused at all, soon went too far. Shrinking from them, but pinned down by them at last, she gave a great deal of the warmth that lay in her. But between their demands upon her, she fancied that she had no sympathy for them at all. She often said that she wished she could be served by machinery.

The door stood open; but amid the breath of the garden, it seemed to me that I could detect, at least I could strongly remember, Lucy's little body odor of blood and honey. The talk of Jean and Eva and Ricketts had carried my imagination again to the Cullen triangle: the virtuous passionate hard-hearted woman, the sad man, and the bird; and I had a new notion. It was that Mrs. Cullen now loved Cullen less than she intended; and lived with him, lived for him, perhaps only to fulfill a dear bootless contract with herself. In any case she loved Lucy, and I hoped she would refuse to give her up.

In the garden, over by the kitchen door, we heard a few notes of mellow laughter. Jean had returned and it had not gone according to Eva's expectation. Laughter, and a rustle and scuffle—the make-believe fighting that when all goes well, relaxes and relieves the true struggle of love—and footsteps diminishing toward the far corner of the garden hidden by the plane trees. The moon that night was not a fine carved shape. It hung under a little loose cloud; only a piece of pallor, a bit of anti-darkness. The air was as warm as Tangier but one could not lie outdoors, I thought, for the grass would be splashed with dew.

"You'll never marry, dear," I said, to tease Alex. "Your friend Mrs. Cullen thinks you will, but she has no imagination. You'll be afraid to, after this fantastic bad luck."

"What bad luck, if you please?" she inquired, smiling to show that my mockery was welcome.

"Fantastic bad object lessons."

"You're no novelist," she said, to tease me. "I envy the Cullens, didn't you know?" And I concluded from the look on her face that she herself did not quite know whether she meant it.

A B O U T   T H E   T Y P E

The text of this book has been set in Trump Mediaeval. Designed by
Georg Trump for the Weber foundry in the late 1950s, this typeface is a
modern rethinking of the Garalde Oldstyle types (often associated with
Claude Garamond) that have long been popular with printers and book
designers.

Trump Mediaeval is a trademark of
Linotype-Hell AG and/or its subsidiaries

Printed and bound by R. R. Donnelley & Sons,
Harrisonburg, Virginia

TITLES IN SERIES

HINDOO HOLIDAY
MY DOG TULIP
MY FATHER AND MYSELF
WE THINK THE WORLD OF YOU
J. R. Ackerley

THE LIVING THOUGHTS OF KIERKEGAARD
W. H. Auden, editor

SEVEN MEN
Max Beerbohm

PRISON MEMOIRS OF AN ANARCHIST
Alexander Berkman

A MONTH IN THE COUNTRY
J. L. Carr

HERSELF SURPRISED (First Trilogy, Volume 1)
TO BE A PILGRIM (First Trilogy, Volume 2)
THE HORSE'S MOUTH (First Trilogy, Volume 3)
Joyce Cary

PEASANTS AND OTHER STORIES
Anton Chekhov

THE PURE AND THE IMPURE
Colette

A HOUSE AND ITS HEAD
MANSERVANT AND MAIDSERVANT
Ivy Compton-Burnett

THE WINNERS
Julio Cortázar

MEMOIRS
Lorenzo Da Ponte

A HANDBOOK ON HANGING
Charles Duff

THE HAUNTED LOOKING GLASS
Edward Gorey, editor

A HIGH WIND IN JAMAICA
THE FOX IN THE ATTIC (The Human Predicament, Volume 1)
THE WOODEN SHEPHERDESS (The Human Predicament, Volume 2)
Richard Hughes

THE OTHER HOUSE
Henry James

THE GLASS BEES
Ernst Jünger

THE WASTE BOOKS
Georg Christoph Lichtenberg